REDEMPTION
CENTER

REDEMPTION CENTER

· stories ·

VINCENT CRAIG WRIGHT

BEAR STAR PRESS

2 0 0 6

10 9 8 7 6 5 4 3 2 1

BEAR STAR PRESS
185 Hollow Oak Drive
Cohasset, California 95973
www.bearstarpress.com

Grateful acknowledgment is made to
the following magazines, where some of these
stories first appeared in slightly different forms:
*The Chattahoochee Review, Georgia Guardian,
Lime Tea, The Point, Short Story, Southern,
West Wind Review, Yemmessee*

Cover design by Charles Grace
with inspiration from Mitch Wyatt and Pat Reinbolt
Book design by Beth Spencer
Author photograph by Simeon Schatz

ISBN: 0-9719607-8-X
Library of Congress Control Number: 2005939110

For Vincent Love, Kenya Sun, Silas Henry,
and their mothers, Christina Drew and Natalie Ann.

And for my mother, my father, my sister,
both paws, granny and grandmama, and my aunt.

"One day I will save the world."
Vincent Love Wright

CONTENTS

THE CHANGING LIGHT

The light changed and he never even slowed down. He went through, and watched the other side, flat red, tremble in his rear-view.

He thought about the stop light where he grew up, how his mom tried to show him a rabbit's shadow in the yellow. Like everything, he told the bartender, the light changed too fast.

Once, though, at an art gallery full of Jackson Pollocks and Frank Stellas, he realized he'd been looking for the wrong shape of rabbit the whole time and felt so sorry for his mother he went into the first strip bar he came to and spent fifty-five dollars in forty-five minutes.

He told the bartender it's how you look at things.

He watched the red light in the mirror until it was a pin prick in the glass, a little spot of dried blood, until one would argue over the shade of red.

And you don't come to expect a posse of bicyclists, fluorescent yellow and green streaks with their own rules, veering at each flank, banking, screaming purple faces, a shiny black shoe kicking the side of the passenger door. You don't learn to expect that.

He was hard on the brakes and there was no making sense of the orange-vested, orange-flag-waving blonde woman in blue jeans, or the orange cone flying over the windshield, or the circular thumping at one wheel.

Then a steamroller, steamrolling.

One of the bicyclists wobbling up on his pedals giving the finger in the reflection.

He hit a curb or a hole, something jarred the radio up loud, and the song was, "Just my Imagination," and he remembered how his mother loved the Temptations except "Papa Was a Rolling Stone."

He remembered the time his daddy'd called the day after his birthday, and the kind of familiar voice said, "I love you," and he'd wondered how does he know.

He remembered the remembering.

The fleshy face of a woman he felt he'd seen before flashed and filled a passing window. She put him in mind of ice skating at six, maybe seven, his mother watching over coffee, her smile more warming than six, maybe seven, sunshines.

He told the bartender about this once and the bartender told him everybody's mother's smile is like that, then thought a minute and said, no, that's not the case, is it? "Wouldn't be all these wars and shit," he said, and threw an ashtray into the garbage overhand.

Sliding in his car, he felt on top of things. If there was nothing he could do, there was nothing he could do, he knew, and he let go, and it didn't surprise him, the wheel turning on its own.

Once, when his dad had been there for some reason, he'd gone along to the car wash where they were pulled through water jets, spinning brushes, and dangling, clinging fabric.

And the steering wheel turned on its own.

He'd reached over and grabbed the wheel and it jerked clean from his fingers. His daddy laughed like an older brother.

They'd stopped for hamburgers on the way home and he studied how his daddy ate, how he took bites and chewed, how he swallowed and everything looked hard going down.

His dad held his hamburger one-handed and steered with his other wrist rested on the wheel, and even with his knee when he reached for a drink of his soda or a french fry or to change the radio.

He felt, in his hips, his back wheels coming around in front of him and even thought to look to his left to see the light directly but couldn't.

He couldn't remember ever getting more than a glance.

One bicyclist stopped near a flag-waver, who held up a cone like a cheerleader's bullhorn. He wondered had anybody ever cheered him for anything.

He knew he was the worst thing she could imagine, but he looked for her, looked to her for something, and she was gone.

The steamroller wasn't rolling any more.

He remembered the face of the woman he'd seen at the window a moment before and wondered what she would say about all this. He thought for a minute he might place her in his past but instead was put in mind of these things from his childhood:

Jots.

The Jungle Book.

Flying fish.

Then the weight of the water.

The stretchy time anesthesia smell falling.

When he felt the start of the soft press into the wall he was relieved at the moment defined. It would end with a crash. It would end like this.

The only thing now was what "it" would be.

What would end with the crash?

What was he going to tell the bartender?

He realized he'd say how everything he knows about life he learned from songs on the radio. It's all there if you listen.

He'd tell the bartender, again, everybody's mom wants to smile like sunshine and warm her children.

With the beginning of the tearing, the jarring and rattling inside, he remembered he could hurt and for the first time how this would've never happened had he stopped at the changing light. This hit him like a brick wall.

At least he hadn't hurt anyone else. He'd know if he hurt somebody else. He'd be able to feel that. And he couldn't feel anything now but his body moving in ways he couldn't get used to.

The crashing reminded him of the crushing crescendo of a holiday orchestra tuning up, little bursts of half-notes and drawn out full-notes moving around and through the chairs, through him, and how the tuning was his favorite part. "That's not even the music," his mother'd said, and he said, "It's all music to me," and she said, "That's just something you heard somewhere," but he believed, then and always, she understood better than that.

He asked his mother did his daddy like music. She said, "Not the way you do," like that was supposed to make him feel good but didn't, but he acted like it did.

Now, with his face flinging for the future faster than the rest of his head, he felt a tug at his soul and remembered and promised himself, again, he'd not forget, again, we have souls.

He liked using the word "we" like this, speaking for the "we" who've gone before, the "we" yet to be, and when your soul all but pulls through the holes in your face you realize you can speak for everybody, and with authority, about the greatest mystery of all.

He remembered the time the light was fever burning in his head and chest and eyes, and when it was sun silvering up on top of the water too long, and he wondered how many times the light behind him changed and the light before him became brighter and the thinking catching up with itself spread into the familiar silver in his eyes until a tunnel opened up for him through.

"So?" she asked.
"What's that?"
"Thought any more about it?"
"About?"
"The whole Lazarus thing."
"Not something I'd recommend," he said.
"You never recommend anything."
"I told you about the Chinese place," he said and put the phone face down into the bed beside him. She'd be home in a matter of minutes.

He smiled at the picture he'd taken when he was little, the black streak, the snake in the air, behind his mom.

She was wading ankle-deep through the rough of the golf course they lived near, looking for lost balls in the grass.

They found a lot some days, none others, and when they did they'd hit most away with the old five-iron they got in a yard sale for a quarter, bring the best home and store them in egg cartons to sell alongside the fairway one day.

And sometimes they'd find the same balls they found before. Sometimes roused a real snake so the one in the picture, hanging in the air, seemed familiar even if it was a blemish as his mother claimed, like that meant anything.

Even years later when his mother'd catch him staring into the picture she'd ask the same question. She'd ask, "What do you see in that snake?"

And he'd say, "The true outlaw."

And she'd ask, "What's that snake doing in my picture?"

He'd say, "Jumping out of himself."

"How's that?"

"Dancing on the heat."

His mom would tell him he should study poetry or something and he'd hold up the picture for her to see.

Sometimes she'd say, "That's a trick of photography."

He wanted to tell her poetry was a trick of words. He wanted to tell her he learned as much looking at that picture as he could in classes and books.

She wanted to take him and go see where he'd wrecked.

She always wanted to go see where he wrecked.

They could be on the way home from seeing where he wrecked and she'd gladly, at any point, turn around and go back and see where he wrecked.

At first, they'd go. She'd stare into the place his car'd hit and say the words the policeman said—"No one survives a wreck like that," and the doctor—"We brought him back."

She'd touch bricks, sometimes leave little notes tucked in cracks.

He never read one though she'd look at him like he ought to at least want to.

She left flowers once, but he told her it made him feel like he was still dead. "I was dead for one minute, twelve seconds," he said to her. "We've been standing here longer than that."

She cried and it wasn't long after that he stopped going with her.

So she gave updates on things that went on at the wall.

"They finished the roadwork," she'd say.

And, "Sometimes when I leave things they're rearranged when

I come back."

Whenever he thought about driving again it never ended good. He liked walking, and would wave at anyone in a window who would wave back. He liked counting steps but never got them to add up to anything.

He told the bartender about his mom and the wall and the dying thing.

The bartender said, "You always think you've heard it all."

"Not me. Not anymore," he said.

"When you were away I couldn't tell you'd died," the bartender said. "Ought to be a way of knowing, a feeling, when someone goes through something like that."

He told the bartender about in third grade when a new kid got hit by a car and nobody in his class knew how to feel, only how they were supposed to feel, how it looked like the teacher felt. Then somebody at recess laughed that laugh that makes kids know everyone's a little wicked on the inside and later on want to go back and do something heroic.

He told his mother, "This morning I dropped a glass on the kitchen floor. When it shattered I felt whole," and wished he hadn't said anything.

She looked at him to say more.

He couldn't imagine what more could be said.

She told him sometimes people just talk.

He agreed. "It's not like you learn more about living from dying. You learn about dying from dying," he said and told her it wasn't what he'd drawn in school when they tried to capture what they were afraid of about death.

He'd colored his whole page black.

The principal called his mother in and asked him in front of her why and he said he'd been asked to do it in art class.

"But I was wrong."

She turned her head and asked, "What then?"

"More a page of light, wrapped out around and away. One without writing," he looked up and said.

His mother brought him a piece of the wall and put it on the mantle beside her picture with the snake in the air. "This might help," she said. "I thought about making a necklace of it but didn't think you'd wear it."

He thought the piece of his past appropriate sitting there between pictures of his grandparents, who didn't die but passed away, all within ten months of each other when he was ten.

He told the bartender about hearing his mom's mom, one day out of the blue, say how she avoided the mirror because it made her feel old, and his grandfather say the mirror didn't scare him, but he insisted all pictures of him be put away.

His mom's mom put the pictures in her old hymnal he'd look through trying to make sense of the gospel words and music staffs, and the pictures of his grandfather would fall into his lap and a few onto the floor.

He told the bartender, wasn't long after that they started passing away.

"All my mom had left," he said, "was me."

The bartender said how everybody's going to die and that's a hell of a thing, isn't it. "Ought to be something you can do."

"There is," he said, "I'll have another." And he told the bartender about the time he fell from four flights and somebody found him, his head resting lightly on the curb.

The time on the bottom of the pool, the light on top of the water bursting into silver splinters like from a song from his mom's mom's hymnal.

He told the bartender how when he was little and only sleeping his mother'd say things like, "I thought you'd never wake up," and he'd lie there looking at her wondering what that would mean until one night he saw in her eyes everything means too much or not enough and decided what he could do for her is not die and how hard that is and easy it can be once you start.

The bartender said, "That's enough."

"That's why I never told her," he said, "but then this thing with the wall."

"In all, there's 1,846 bricks if you count half bricks as halves," his mom told him.

He asked how else you'd count them.

She said she used to think the halves were ends of wholes until she saw the edges of the hole he went into.

"It's all how you look at things," he said.

"Learn something every day," she said.

"I don't," he said. "Not anymore."

A mudslide in ninth grade took out a family everybody thought was perfect. The whole town attended the funeral and kin came from all over the state.

He fell in love with one of the dead kids' cousins and they kissed behind the church, though he never knew her name.

She tasted like potato chips.

She said because she'd been crying, though she didn't know them. "Family and all," she said.

She asked questions about mudslides. She couldn't picture how it could happen.

He told her it's better that way and felt five years older.

They kissed one last time.

He told her when they went on a field trip to Sacramento her cousin that got covered over in mud, the boy, Joel, was his buddy, and they kept up with each other all day through the art museum, and at lunch in the mall food court, and that afternoon when they went to the park. "It was the only time we were friends," he told her, and she cried again.

Her mama came around the corner swinging a baby big enough to walk at her side and said everybody'd been screaming their heads off for her.

She walked away without saying good-bye.

He cried until nobody came looking for him. He walked around front by himself and the church felt bigger from the outside. Adults were standing around smoking cigarettes. Kids were playing in the perfect church grass, but he went inside.

He'd never seen church this empty. One grandmother of the kids who got killed sat in the front pew staring at the big picture of Jesus in the stained glass behind where the preacher stands.

He walked down the aisle and as he got closer heard her talking to the Jesus up there that never looked like any Jesus he'd seen before.

He told the bartender once, "There's as many Jesuses as Santa

Clauses."

He kept toward the grandmother. She rocked gently and wiped at tears.

He looked around for the preacher or somebody, but it was only them and the Jesus.

He never stopped or, he told the bartender more than once, he would've turned around and gone out and played with who'd play with him.

Even when she looked up and saw him, he kept toward her. Even as he heard his name called somewhere, she opened her arms like he was one of hers and he climbed up on her lap and they cried together for so long he forgot who came and got him.

"They're going to tear down the wall," his mother said.

"Old building," he said.

"But that's your wall."

"Seems more like your wall anymore," he said.

She looked at him like he'd given back a present.

"Just something I believe in," she said.

"You believe in that wall?"

"I do."

He said, "It's a brick wall I ran into and happened to live through it."

"You do."

"What's that?"

"You live through that wall."

"I don't know if I could live through dying again," he told her.

"You won't have to," she said.

He wondered did she know what she was saying.

She was there when they knocked down the wall. Bricks tore at her fingernails, but she picked up the pieces and piled them perfectly in the trunk until the car sat all the way down on its haunches.

She had to take out some and put them on the front floorboard to close the trunk and drove around that way while she figured out what to do.

When he first saw what she was doing he cried like on the dead kids' grandmother's lap.

He wanted his mother to stop and come inside and catch him that way, but she kept laying bricks according to what she'd see when she'd close her eyes and what she'd read from some big book with bits of broken bricks holding open the pages.

The beginning grew up out of the middle of their back yard.

She had her trowel and her wheelbarrow of mortar and her hose run out to her like she built walls in their back yard every day.

He watched until she didn't come in.

He went out and took her a glass of water. Then sat her down on a lawn chair, took the trowel, and worked on the wall. When he finished, in the changing light of time, he took pictures of her standing in front of the wall, and set the timer and got in one with her, and they smiled without anybody telling them, and the prints came out perfect, and the wall's still standing, keeping nothing out and nothing in.

LOOKING OUT FOR RITA

Was neither of us surprised she hadn't showed up yet, it being Rita.

Still, we acted that way until the guy drove up, got out and handed me and Danny the first two beers from his twelve-pack, sat down on his bumper, opened himself a beer and started talking.

Something happened with the guy's girlfriend and his brother or half brother, I couldn't figure it out.

"Know what I'm saying?" the guy'd ask.

We said yeah, we knew what he was saying.

"I can't believe she'd do that to me. Know what I'm saying?" he'd say, even when it wasn't hard to tell what he was saying.

After a while we'd nod.

He'd found out that morning and spent the whole day driving on it and he kept talking until we didn't nod when he'd ask did we know what he was saying.

When we finished the beer Danny broke out his bottle of birthday gin and we drank, the guy talking, us not nodding or saying anything anymore.

Then, about halfway down the bottle, Danny told the guy, "It don't fit together the way you tell it."

The guy agreed but maintained that's what he was saying. It wasn't the way he was telling it but the way it happened. "Know what I'm saying?" he asked like never before.

After the gin nobody went for more to drink.

I watched an airplane fly over. I wondered about people up in the sky, flying for the reasons people fly. I wondered where was Rita.

The guy told us again the situation between his two-week girlfriend and, I finally figured out, his stepbrother from when their parents got married when he was eighteen. Again, the guy said know what I'm saying, and got where that's all he'd say, until Danny said, "I know what you're saying, but it's bullshit."

"Bullshit?" the guy asked.

"Every bit," Danny said.

The guy looked concerned. He looked at me. Then down at the empty twelve-pack at his feet.

Then, something Danny'd do drunk, he reached out with his foot and barely kicked over the empty twelve-pack.

I hadn't thought about it up to then, but the guy was bigger than Danny, both of them bigger than me, and I thought how I'd been dealing with pissed-off, bigger-than-me people my whole life.

Danny said, "Know what I'm saying?" Then nudged the empty twelve-pack on top of the guy's foot.

Another airplane going by felt like nobody up there but the pilot on his way home and I wondered would Rita show up.

The guy didn't move his eyes when Danny nudged the twelve-pack. He kept looking at the spot where it had been. Then, the same thing he'd been saying the whole time, but this time said it more than asked, and right to the spot where the empty twelve-pack had been, "You know what I'm saying."

"Let me explain something to you," Danny told him. "Fuck you."

One of the prettiest girls I'd ever known, Claire Gibson, rode by with her dad in a brand new blue Buick and she waved at me but stopped once she took in everything.

While I'm watching her dad's car swerve around something in the road, the guy snatches the empty twelve-pack off his foot, stands up and steps toward Danny, throws the thing overhand like he used to be a pitcher, right into Danny's face.

Danny went over to the guy's car and kneeled.

Danny loved to tell, especially when Rita was around, how some dude his daddy knew fought with the little end of the pool stick so people'd feel it, or how this girl we went to school with beat up her mama's ex-boyfriend with his own shoe when she woke up and he was in her bed, and Danny'd swear how some other dude sword-fought three bikers with a broke-off car antenna.

I figured one day he'd try this sort of thing so it didn't surprise me, him on a knee working at the guy's antenna.

The guy stood there, trying to figure out what Danny was doing to his car.

We both watched for what seemed like a long time but wasn't, I don't think. Then Danny bent the antenna over about 45 degrees and the guy looks at me like I ought to understand what he's about to do, which I do, and the guy goes over and smacks Danny right in the back of the neck with the fleshy part of his hand.

Danny turned around and I thought, now it's a fight, but he looks at the guy like a new friend. He had the antenna behind his back, working it back and forth, trying to snap it off, still smiling at the guy.

When the guy saw Danny still hanging onto his antenna he half-swung again, like he made himself, but his fist got caught in Danny's shirt collar and long hair.

They stood looking at each other, the guy's fingers in Danny's hair, Danny still working the guy's antenna and smiling.

I went over and put my hands on them like I knew what to do.

They looked at me, waiting. They looked at each other. There was something needed to be done.

I reached over and straightened up the guy's antenna. It wasn't perfect, but everything seemed good.

Another airplane flew over.

Some deep-voiced girl drove by in a little banged-up, black pickup with the tail-gate missing, and yelled, "Y'all going to fight or fuck?"

I felt what she'd said running through us. I reached over and tried to straighten out the antenna the rest of the way and it broke off in my hand.

I wasn't sure what the guy was going to do.

Danny looked at me with the antenna in my hand like I had all the power in the world.

I closed my eyes.

I remembered watching *Zorro* in my mama's recovered-for-Christmas corduroy chair. By the end of the show I'd grab one arm and run circles, spinning the chair along with me. When I couldn't run any longer from being out of breath, I'd sling the arm of the chair ahead of me and watch it spin by until I'd jump on and ride off like Zorro'd be doing on TV. I'd hold up the flyswatter or whatever I was using for a sword that day and ride all the way to a stop.

When I opened my eyes the guy was still standing there.

I handed him his antenna.

Danny looked back and forth between us.

The guy looked back and forth between his antenna and where it had been attached to his car.

Then he got down on a knee.

He closed one eye and tried sticking his antenna back onto the jagged nub sticking up out of his car. He held both pieces together tight in the same hand he'd had on Danny's neck, like the pieces might weld together somehow from the sweat and heat and pressure from his fist, and used his other hand up high, straightening.

Even though it felt like me and Danny weren't there anymore I could tell from my angle the pieces weren't quite lined up. Part of me'd still wish, each time he'd look, somehow, that the antenna'd be stuck back on good as new.

He'd peek into his fist, squint, and cuss when he wouldn't have them straight. A lot of times the two pieces wouldn't even be touching.

I put my arm around Danny and took him inside to see if there was anything we could scrape up to smoke. That's when I realized I would've been the one going to jail had the cops come. They take the guy with his shirt off. We know from TV and from experience that sorting things out isn't something they're interested in when there's a guy with his shirt off.

So I felt lucky to be free in that moment and a sense of goodness ran through me from how I stopped a big fight even though we ended up breaking the guy's antenna.

Danny dug through ashtrays and the corners of old baggies. I looked a little but knew we were wasting time, so when I found an old sticky roll of duct tape in the kitchen cabinet I took it out to the guy. He seemed appreciative. He said the car'd been his uncle's before he'd died or he wouldn't've got so upset. That, and the thing about his girlfriend and how Danny didn't know what he was saying.

I told him Danny knew what he was saying and that was the problem.

Rita'd been supposed to get her tattoo fixed, pick up Chinese food, then Danny, and take him to get some pot. Wouldn't none of that happened with the guy and his antenna and the empty twelve-pack had Rita showed up.

Instead, she'd called from her mom's.

"She's thinking about going back to her husband," Danny said like he had to tell me that.

"Was he there?" I asked him. Rita's husband, Jon Diamond, lived with Rita's mom as roommates.

"He's giving a seminar at the community center," Danny said.

Jon Diamond was trying to catch on as a fitness guru, developing his game locally, doing community center things where they charged eight dollars an hour for the building if you cleaned up after your event.

I reminded Danny how Rita's parents, who were still together at the time, rented the place for Rita's graduation party even though she didn't graduate. Everybody found that out when Rita's brother Butch got thrown out of his own sister's graduation party for being a narc, then stood outside yelling, "The bitch ain't graduating," until you had to believe him, and their dad went out with a piece of hose he snatched off the ice machine and had to pay for later.

But it wasn't that Danny thought Rita might get back with her husband.

It wasn't the Chinese food he was pissed off about when the guy stopped with the twelve-pack, and it wasn't that we drank up his birthday gin.

Danny didn't smoke much more than anybody else but had to have it around. He'd start looking way before he ran out and only ran out when things got real dry, like in the middle of summer.

He kept trying to light this roach he found under a Fruit Loops box while he told me for the hundredth time how Rita got the pot now because Butch narced on Frederick who was going to kick Butch's ass until Rita went to see him. Nobody talks about what happened, but her brother didn't get beat up and Rita'd been getting the pot ever since. It wasn't great, but it'd get you high.

Of course, Danny only liked her going over there last resort.

Sometimes she'd come back with a buzz but no pot and Danny'd throw things.

"Freddy don't feel good about people just coming and going," she'd say.

We never heard anyone call him Freddy.

Danny asked her couldn't she work out some code and just call.

"He don't like talking on the phone," she said. "That ain't cool."

Danny knew that. She had him there.

So this time she was going to pick up Danny and let him wait down the block. Except she hadn't showed up.

Without him getting more than a pissed-off hit, the roach burned up in Danny's fingers. He watched out the window at the guy. Said he might go back out there.

I wasn't sure what to do.

Sometimes in life there's a ring around something like the sun, or the ring of some far-away horn or bell, and sometimes you recognize the ring for what it is and people say saved by the bell or whatever. This time it was the telephone with my friend Kenny Ray from a band we tried to start when we were kids, wanting to help somebody down the coast a ways unload a quarter pound of big bud.

When Danny figured out what we were talking about on the phone he said, "Fuck Rita," grinning like his life was fair.

I told Kenny Ray bring the shit on over.

"I knew you'd be all about that big bud, dog," Kenny Ray said. "That's why I went ahead and sent my boy by to see you."

"I guess that's cool," I told him, looking out the window at the guy still peeking into his fist at his broken antenna. It reminded me of Danny finding this little bird when we were like twelve and how he kept peeking in his hand and breathing in there to keep the little thing warm and made a nest out of string and sticks in a shoebox until the bird was old enough to fly. Watching the bird fly out of Danny's upheld hands that day stays with me and gives me hope, not only for Danny but somehow for the whole world, but part of me holds back just a little of that hope, just in case.

I asked Kenny Ray, "When's he coming?"

"Ought to be there soon's what I'm saying," Kenny Ray said, "if he ain't stopped off at some bar drinking himself sideways. My man's all upset about his girl fucking his brother or some crazy shit."

I said, "You're kidding."

He said, "Fucked up what people do to each other, ain't it?"

I told him it was.

Through the window the guy was trying to crimp one end of the antenna so it'd fit inside the other.

Danny's old numchucks held open the window and I thought how I was glad the antenna hadn't come off all smoothly where Danny would've been in that Kung-Fu zone and started slashing at the guy with it.

"The dude'll talk you to death and shit," Kenny Ray said on the phone, "but he's got the real-deal big bud."

When I hung up I asked Danny did he think the guy'd still sell the quarter pound to us.

"Hell yeah, he's going to sell it to us," he said, up on his toes looking out at the guy laying across the hood of his car with one eye closed.

But Danny never has money. Not quarter-pound kind of money.

I damn sure didn't have it.

"He'll have to front it to us," Danny said.

"You fucked up his uncle's car," I reminded him.

"I don't know his uncle and his uncle ain't got the pot," Danny said like it made sense. "Business is business, isn't it?"

I said business was business, then told him how the guy's uncle died.

Danny said, "I'll talk to him."

"Don't fuck it up," I said but already felt like it was too late, like I was saying something so I could say I said so later.

When Danny and I were ten, we figured out each of our parents thought we were spending the night with the other one. Wasn't nothing we planned, just worked out that way, our first opportunity, and we decided to seize upon it. And Danny fucked it up.

We were thirteen and these fourteen-year-old girls from out of town wanted to sneak out and come see us. We were camping out in his fort and we had four beers. Danny fucked that up, too.

I had my driver's license and Danny didn't yet. We snuck Mom's car out and were just driving, really not doing much but rolling down the windows and turning up the radio and feeling free for the first time in our little lives. He fucked that up.

So I decided to watch Danny talk to the guy from the window. He wouldn't let me, though. He pulled me by the arm. He surprised me and said, "I might fuck it up."

Something in that brought real tears to my eyes, thinking about us there always in the middle of these things with the whole world wrapped around us, and how the air we were walking around in blows around all sorts of people though it doesn't feel like it does. In that moment I couldn't imagine things for all the people in the world to do. There didn't seem like enough for me and Danny to do, even with this ahead of us, trying to talk the guy into fronting us the quarter pound of big bud.

"Are you crying, motherfucker?" Danny asked me. He knew me to be sensitive about things that didn't bother other people, and he knew I wasn't crying because I was scared of the guy, that if I was scared of anything it was big things we don't have control over. He knew that. He'd listened to me trying to figure out stuff under enough different circumstances and highs, he knew. Him asking me, "Are you crying, motherfucker?" was his way of checking in, making sure I was all right. Which I was. Things just get overwhelming sometimes when I think about them.

One time I tried to quit cussing. I thought I'd sound smarter but ended up searching so long around my head for a way to put something I didn't want to say it anymore.

When we got out there the guy had duct-taped his antenna together and was checking his reception, which wasn't bad, I didn't think, but I didn't have anything to compare it to.

He couldn't decide. He was running through stations and

turning each ear toward each speaker.

"I can get another antenna for your car," Danny said.

The guy kept checking stations like he couldn't hear anything.

"Not that hard to put one back on," Danny said, peeling up the edge of the duct tape until he realized what he was doing, smoothing it back out with the back of his fingernail and a little smile, moving his head around like he was making sure the guy's antenna was on straight.

I told the guy how I'd heard from Kenny Ray, but he kept tuning his radio.

"We could pay you for something like that by tomorrow," I said. "Wouldn't be any problem."

The guy stopped on a song I'd never heard. He turned it up and put his head back on the headrest, closed his eyes and listened to the song. When the song was over I didn't know if I would recognize it if I ever heard it again.

Danny was one of those where every song meant something about something. He could tell you what was playing at Rita's graduation party, or any other night where something happened, but there's so much music and other stuff playing in my head it's hard for me to know when anything else means anything.

The guy opened his eyes, turned down the radio a little and said, "That's a good song."

Danny nodded that it was.

I thought that was good, how they had something in common.

I said, "Would you be into something like that? Letting us hold onto that until tomorrow?"

"A damn good song," the guy said. "Know what I'm saying?"

Danny cut his eyes at me, but I acted like I didn't see.

"We could turn something like that around pretty quick," I said. "Have your money for you tomorrow like I said."

"I got a grip on all you fellows could handle," he said, but looked at Danny and added, "I don't know how I feel about it, though."

I looked at Danny like I was saying, "See there."

Danny said, "Man, I didn't know," like he meant it, like that was supposed to make some difference.

The guy looked straight up into Danny's face and said, "You

didn't know what I was saying."

"That's not what I meant," Danny said, more to me than the guy.

"The whole time," the guy said.

"You want to come in?" I asked because I couldn't think of anything else to say, and I needed to. "Might be a little something to eat."

Wasn't shit to eat.

"Would like to use your phone," he said, rubbing his face and rolling the back of his head around on his headrest.

I knew he was thinking about his girl then.

A plane went over and he said, "Damn, you live close to a airport?"

I told him we did.

"I knew," I told him.

"You knew what?" He leaned over and opened his glove compartment and was digging through it, feeling around.

"I knew what you were saying," I said.

He looked at me, still leaned over with his hand in the glove box under some papers.

Danny was trying to see what was in the glove box.

"Wasn't much chance to tell you before, with everything going on," I told him, "but I knew. I knew what you were saying the whole time."

He looked out the windshield like he was watching what'd happened with the empty twelve-pack and him and Danny and his antenna. He put his left hand up on top of the steering wheel and looked like he was driving the same road all of us been down.

He looked like he was in that song he liked.

After a few miles that way he said, "What is it about women?"

Danny smiled, because he knew I had the guy.

Because he knows I know what it is with women.

Same way I know what it is with God and death and what ought to be done about abortion and war and all that stuff everybody wants answers to.

I knew what he was saying, and I know all that other stuff like what it is with women, because every answer to every question, every one if you know how to look for them, is piled up with all the others in every *Reader's Digest* my Aunt Ella ever saved, which was every one printed between June of '50 and August of '81 save the few I always wondered what happened to.

I said, "Can we at least go in and sit down and puff a bowl, the three of us, try and act like we're on the same side here?" Meaning us men on this side trying to figure out women and all that.

"Women," Danny said like he was catching on, but as always he was close to fucking up.

When Danny saw the pot he let out a breath that reminded me of somebody on a nature show watching baby animals being born, reminded me of him and the little bird.

The guy held up this huge bud, twirled it a little, and said, "You know what I'm saying now, huh, motherfucker," but was smiling so everything felt all right, like we were on the same side.

But when he packed the bowl, he was one of those that sat there holding it, talking. When he did finally light the thing he sat there holding it some more, talking, letting the smoke out of his mouth with what he was saying.

He told us how he met his girlfriend or used-to-be girlfriend, he wasn't sure yet. She'd been coming out of the library and he'd stopped his car in the middle of the street because not only was she pretty but coming out of the library made him think she was smart. He didn't much like to read, but he liked girls that did, he said. "Turned out she was returning romance novels for her mom," he told us, "but I gave her a ride home anyway and we started hanging out."

Danny watched the pipe in his hand. The smell of the smoke had him jonesing even worse than before. Me, too, and the guy was waving the pipe around like something he needed to make his point.

Danny's eyes followed the whole way. I knew he wouldn't last long, that this was a perfect opportunity for Danny to fuck up getting a quarter pound of the best pot to come through in a while, all because he was jonesing for a hit. He was following the pipe in the guy's hand with his whole head now.

I said, "How's that stuff taste?" and nodded toward the guy's hand.

He said it tasted real nice. Then looked at me. "Know what I'm saying?"

I didn't even look at Danny. I was a little scared to, thinking about the empty twelve-pack and all.

The guy looked at each of us and took another hit. He leaned back and closed his eyes, blew the smoke straight up into the air until it hit the ceiling and spread across the top of the room. He kept his head back and eyes closed that way, the pipe hanging there between his fingers not a foot away from Danny's hand.

Danny looked at me and I knew enough to shake my head no.

"It's been a while since we've had pot smell that good around here," I said like I meant it because I did.

Danny said, in a nice way, "Sure has," and it took everything for him to leave it at that and I was proud. The guy banged the ashes out on the coffee table and packed another bowl and I thought, okay, this one's for me and Danny, and I looked at Danny like that.

Then the guy started telling a story about his stepbrother and how they were going in on buying this piece-of-shit car together so they could fix it up and resell it and damned if he doesn't take another hit off his pipe right there in front of us, sucking on the thing and shifting his eyes back and forth through the flame, the son of a bitch, and I decided it didn't matter if I pissed him off, and said, "Danny, do we have any marijuana we could offer this man?"

He said, "No."

"Because I was thinking we were going to smoke together, all of us, try and talk a little business." I looked square at the guy and said, pronouncing pretty good, "Know what I'm saying?"

The guy didn't open his eyes, sat there like in his own chair in his own house, and looked like at any minute he might ask what's for dinner, yet he held onto that pipe like people don't pass around the pipe when they smoke at his house, like they just sit there like some stupid son of a bitch in their chair and don't pass around the pipe.

I said, again, "Know what I'm saying?" And wished for the empty twelve-pack.

The guy took another hit, not in any hurry either. It occurred to me he might have a gun, but I didn't feel like he did, especially with everything that already happened.

The phone rang and I let it. I tried to let each ring mean something until Kenny Ray came on the answering machine wanting to know did the guy ever show up and how everything worked out. He said, "Whatever you do, don't let Danny piss him off because I've seen my man do some crazy shit," right where we all heard it. "Cold, calculating bastard," Kenny Ray said.

The guy smiled.

I said, "Well?" And held my hands open like I hadn't heard what everybody else had, like I hadn't been there the whole time and seen everything with the empty twelve-pack, and heard the message. "Can we try the product?" I asked.

The guy looked at the pipe like for the first time. Looked at me. Then Danny.

Then Rita pulled up out front.

We watched through the window while she got out of her car.

The first time me and Danny saw Rita we were 15, at the swimming pool, hanging onto the edge talking. She walked through the gate in blue jeans and a sweat shirt over her swim suit. We watched her undress like there was nothing else happening in the whole world.

While she pulled off her blue jeans we could neither one say a word.

Even though she had on her bikini Danny said there wasn't much difference and sure enough she stood there like she was in her orange underwear until I had to go under water and hold my breath as long as I could. When I came back up she was in midair, diving over the top of me. Then she was gone and Danny said, "That's going to be my girlfriend one day."

It took a while, but she was. She was all of our girlfriend one time or another, or that's what we thought.

Even when she married Jon Diamond she didn't act married, and nobody expected her to by then. We expected her to be Rita, which she was, day in and day out. Even as she got older and the younger dudes didn't always see her that way, she didn't need any help being Rita.

The guy smiled when he saw Rita coming to the door.

Danny turned his head at a weird angle.

Rita came in cussing about where the guy had parked until she saw him sitting there with us.

The guy was making some kind of clicking sound with his mouth and when I looked at him he yawned like he was making himself do it.

Then he passed Rita the pipe.

She took a huge hit.

Danny had his mouth open.

After she blew out the smoke she took another hit. Maybe she thought we'd been sitting smoking together all along and was trying to catch up. When she blew the smoke out, she held out the pipe and said, "Who's this go to?"

She was Rita a hundred per cent standing there with the guy's pipe in her hand, like he was the only person in the room with her, asking who the pipe goes to like she was saying something else.

Sure e-damn-nough, the guy reached for the pipe.

Danny shifted around on the couch like he was heavier than he was.

I said, "We were about to talk a little business," like maybe Rita'd leave before things got worse. I knew better, though, in my heart, and I knew it sounded that way when I said it.

She looked at the guy, nodded at his pipe and said, "Can I get a fresh hit of that, you think?"

"Sure," the guy said like he was the most sharing motherfucker, period, and stuck a bud in the pipe, mashed it in deep with his thumb and handed her the pipe and lighter in one hand.

She took it in both hers and gave both Danny and me enough of a glance I thought she might know what she was doing. I started to say something but realized I'd know for sure once she hit the bowl. If she handed it back to the guy, she knew what she was doing for sure, was definitely fucking with me and Danny, and if she passed it to one of us everything was all right.

Then she did the same thing the guy did. She stood there holding the pipe. Danny kept looking at her, trying to catch her eye. He wanted her to sit down by him on the couch, hand over the bowl.

She wasn't saying anything, just standing there with us all

looking at her and I realized that was all she wanted, to be looked at, and I realized that a lot of the time in our lives that's all we wanted to do, or at least all we did, look at Rita.

After that night, Danny'd try to tell somebody what happened and they never believed him. Even with it being Rita everybody thought we were making it up, or adding to it. For a while Danny'd nod at me to support his story, but I never liked talking about it.

It started with Rita's cell phone. Jon Diamond wanted to know where she was, what she was doing, when she'd be home. Which was another thing, how Rita usually stayed with her sister or Danny but still kept most her stuff at her mom's, and Jon Diamond always called it her home like if he kept after it eventually she'd live there with him and her mom like family.

We all kept looking at her while she talked on the phone. I filled in what Jon Diamond was saying based on what she said and what I knew about men around Rita.

I knew she was in her element.

I thought about how I wouldn't know my element if I was in the middle of it, then I thought, no, this was my element too, looking at Rita.

Then she hung up her phone and took off her shirt.

Caught us all off guard. She had on one of those sports bras some women wear like they have on shirts, but it still seemed like a bra to me. "It's hot," she said.

"Sure is," the guy said, and Danny moved around on the couch again.

"Wish we had something to drink," she said.

"We all wish," the guy said. "Know what I'm saying? No matter what we have or what comes true, we keep on wishing."

Rita looked at him like he made sense.

"Know what I'm saying?" he asked.

Danny said, "I'm tired of this," like he was talking about our whole lives as much as the situation there, and he jumped up and reached to take the pipe from Rita.

That's when she did what nobody believes.

Started crying. She sat down and cried like the little girl she must've been before we knew her. Even when Danny wrestled the pipe out of her hand and took a hit he could barely hold and rushed the pipe over to me, she kept crying a big cry from way down her back.

The guy reached over and stuck a bud in the pipe for me and Danny. "Sometimes I don't know what I'm saying," he said.

We sat there smoking that way, letting Rita cry, trying not to look at her in her bra, and when she slowed down a little Danny went and got his blue jean jacket and wrapped it around her and we watched her wipe her eyes and smile.

Must've been a year after that Jon Diamond left to go to L.A. Me and Rita moved in together the next week.

Didn't seem like there was anything left to do by then.

One day I saw Danny walking down the road and I started to stop, but I didn't. I knew he saw me, but I kept going.

Two weeks later I saw him again so I had to stop. We sat on the hood of the car and he told me how he was Assistant Pro at the golf course now. "You don't really have to be a good golfer to work in the shop," he said.

I told him I had to get going. "She rides home this way," I said.

He asked how things were going with Rita.

An airplane went over and I didn't have to say anything, it being Danny.

HOUSE OF WOOD

Ever since the dead man looked at Mattie our town has become a sort of bird sanctuary.

The town council never decreed our town a sanctuary, but birds began landing on the backs of the slow-moving, and the feeling was that harming even one of the birds would lock us into good weather through the millennium.

The council discussed building Mattie's house from unnecessary umbrellas, but Mattie's mother, who came here after a war no one ever heard of, said no, Mattie always dreamed of living in a house of wood.

Most of us already had enough reason to talk about Mattie and the way she walks without word getting out she was wooed by wood.

It took an act of God and Mattie's mother to get the dead man buried. Surely he's seen enough by now, she said, her own gaze tied to the horizon by a string of jays.

Crows, gathered at the dead man's grave then chased away by the wren who keeps vigil there even now, keeps the dirt loose and cool above the dead man, clouded into a corner of the sky.

The day after the dead man looked at Mattie, she walked through town, birds bunching on the brick about her, and she took down our flag, went home and made a dress of it, the likes of which we haven't seen since the man with the green trunk left to join the tea trade.

Mattie's mother married a sideshow strongman she met shaving outside his tent.

Story has it he owned no mirror so shaved from memory. That the next morning Mattie's mother brought him a piece of mirror. That when he looked into it he cried.

The next day, as the carnival wiggled away, we all waved at Mattie's mother on the strongman's wagon.

Two years later she came home. With Mattie. No one was weak enough to ask.

Mattie never went to school. Stayed out by quizzing anyone on whatever subject they claimed expertise. Our mayor, who'd majored in mathematics at a university, once managed to engage Mattie in the possibility of attending until she asked about the multiplying of hungry children, the dividing of the human race. It doesn't add up, she said.

Our flag, Mattie's dress, hung so you couldn't see the X tattooed in the flesh between her thumb and forefinger. You had to suppose it was there.

The entrance to Mattie's room in her mother's house smelled of fresh tobacco and melting candle wax, and sheets of light shifted when she'd open the shaky door.

She grew garlic and sold it at market, trading cloves left at the end of the day for plums and pomegranates.

Her singing on Sundays saved us from having to buy a new church bell. She played saxophone on Saturday nights, saying to a group of ladies gathered on her doorstep in protest how the one balanced the other. In some ways, she said, it gives me a place to sing from.

From then on we detected a particular beauty in her saxophone music though some said it was an acquired taste and a committee formed to look into church bells.

The day it rained, clearly an act of God since no weatherman saw it coming, Mattie's mother buried the dead man, telling the gravediggers the dirt was finally soft enough for their shovels.

No one noticed when the diggers hit hard dirt because we were all making brick, the children gathering water falling from the sky in bottles and buckets so we could make more brick in the days following.

And brick after brick baked day after day until Mattie applied for her building permit and someone heard her mother say how Mattie'd prefer a house of wood.

The town council remembered the rain of the dead man's burial like a birthday promise and suggested Mattie just build her house from our useless umbrellas. There wasn't much brick, they argued. It should mark the dead man's grave. And no one built a house of wood in our town.

The birds, they decided by a close vote, were here for the weather.

The final business of the meeting concerned Mattie's new dress.

They decided quickly that she should make it back into a flag to be raised above the town again before church come Sunday.

All day Saturday Mattie gave away garlic. Only took pomegranates and plums she could eat then and there. She smiled her same smile of sailing ships and salt shakers, and she moved through the birds like she was wading in from the ocean, waves nipping the back of her knees.

That evening many of us thought there was a special event at the church until word spread shop to shop how the singing was coming from Mattie's mother's house, from the entrance to Mattie's room where the light from the candles, some whispered, was the same as always.

It rained that night, though most of us thought we were dreaming of the rain that came the day they buried the dead man.

Next morning, the echoes of Mattie's singing still damp and sparkling, the absence of birds in the air sounded to many of us like a church bell so we went to church.

We sat frozen in Reverend's fiery eyes.

Perched in our pews like each of us knew the same secret but couldn't tell.

We tried to figure out what Reverend was talking about.

We all knew our flag was out there flying.

We prayed.

When the saxophone started, and when we found ourselves out front of the church and there was Mattie in the rain, sheltered by a cross of brick and covered in birds, her sax spitting out clay, we knew the dead man had been right to look at her.

Mattie got her house of wood, though most women quit wearing their best to church because of it.

And the church became popular with our young people. On odd Saturdays, the first and third of each month, they'd hold dances and you could hear Mattie's sax stick to the stained glass like she was wrapping the place in half notes.

The man with the green trunk came back, its hinges straining, and Mattie's mother bought the first dress to spring out and walked to Mattie's house and gave it to her.

Most of the birds had been forgotten.

The rest lived at Mattie's house.

Women would bring things to Mattie, maybe a music box or a piece of cloth, and they'd stand in her house and run their hands down the wood like it was the face of a reincarnated lover, maybe a lieutenant in the army of some queen.

Later they'd circle together and try to believe stories about the woman who kept lovers in the grain and splinter of her home.

Brick pews were planned for the church, but since they had to be built inside, and most of our men felt bad working in the church, we sat on the floor on Sundays and most of our women wouldn't wear their best dress.

And at the end of a service, when Mattie'd start her song, everyone would shift a little on the dirt and think of the last Sunday we had pews, when we walked out not to the singing, not to the saxophone, but to Mattie crucified bird to brick, and the men of our town, following a common impulse, began to pull up the pews and the children carried them down, one by one, to Mattie's place.

Built her house of wood.

TELLING TIME

J ohn Bratton was trying to shoot straight on this, what he somehow decided was his last day.

Trying things like, "Listen, the best thing for you is hang up before the end of this minute."

And when the customer protested, he'd say, "Okay, that's what I see. You will not call these sorts of places. You will begin to believe in yourself."

A few cussed him right out, but the rest, in some way, could hear in his voice what they probably already suspected.

One thought he was trying to sell him some new how-to-quit-your-psychic program.

After one of his calls, he looked over and said, "The thing best about knowing you're going to die like this, the day at hand and all, is, and this is for John Bratton, the thing best is the way light looks. Anywhere. Just the way it looks. Like baby eyes," he said.

Said he knew this morning last night would be John Bratton's last night to go to sleep.

Calling himself his own name wasn't doing a thing to convince me.

First, he looked the same he did the night before, leaving Teddy's, and second, he's never been psychic before.

Said he was psychic of course, like all of us do, but we don't say that to each other. I mean, goddamn.

So this morning he comes in, tells me he's had this vision of his own death, not how but when, and starts picking up the phone telling customers they're wasting their money and time.

I get my break when he comes in so I hadn't tried taking any calls in the midst of this part preaching, part pleading, part pretty much pissing me right off.

Luckily, the phone don't ring a while so I get a chance to talk sense to him, but he starts going through old client lists and calling them.

"Yes, ma'am, this is John Bratton. Well, I was Jean Bratón when we last spoke, I was even John Bratton then, but listen, I am now calling you on behalf of the United States Psychic Alliance asking that you seek truth in yourself, not a long-distance telephone call."

We work on combined commission. On what we make together.

Our commercials run at the bottom of the hour so between something-fifteen and -thirty's a time to gather together our best lines and pitches, catch our breath with a cigarette.

Not for John, though. Not today.

It was 9:23 and he wasn't breaking stride.

Then he run into some fellow on the phone wasn't going to let him off the hook that easy.

"Sir, John Bratton was a different person then," he kept saying with things like, "I know that's what it says on TV," and, "Sir, it was just a good guess."

Then the fellow asked him something that hung him up a minute, something you didn't see when he was working our side.

Eventually, he said, "Sir, again, luck."

The man said something else.

"Sir, John Bratton's calling lots of his old customers."

Then he sat there listening a while. Looked at me, but I wasn't getting involved.

He said, "Coincidence, sir, pure-t coincidence."

This time the man took a good minute to say what was on his mind. We usually look at those as freebies because the customer's paying $1.99 a minute to tell you things while you sit counting how much you're making. Looking at John, though, it didn't seem like anything was free.

"Sir," he couldn't stand it anymore, cut the fellow off, "I know it seems to you only a psychic would know you took the night off. I realize that's not something you do all that often, but don't you see? I'm calling everybody. If you weren't home the phone would have just kept ringing. Not every one I called tonight was home. What's that tell you, sir? How come I bothered calling them if I could have just known? In fact, sir, if you're okay calling psychic hot lines, if it was doing you any good at all, and I was psychic, wouldn't I know?"

There must have been hesitation because John said, "Seems I got you."

The man still had his own thoughts, though, and John, patient as he was trying to be, must have realized he wasn't going to get very far, that there were more out there he might reach.

"Sir, I'm going let you go. You won't listen to a damn thing I'm telling you. If you'd been this difficult the first time we talked we wouldn't be having to have this conversation. I want you to listen, then I'm hanging up, got me? Life ain't about some great secret, at least not one somebody'll tell you over the phone. Life's living, got me? And I don't mean on a telephone." He kind of looked over at me with that last and hung up like he was a basketball player.

I told him, "Something's got into you."

He said, "Yeah," using that tone people get when they're about to share their testimonial with you, smiling that testimony smile, and I was thinking, well, that makes sense of this, but what he said was, "Life on this planet's one step and I feel my foot coming down."

John's wife left him a year back with one of John's best customers, Manny the Cobbler.

John named him the Cobbler because, from the time Manny started calling and asking John about women, John stayed in nice shoes.

By the time he ever knew he had a name like the Cobbler it didn't bother Manny John had such nice shoes because, by then, Manny the Cobbler had John's wife, Sophronia.

Once Sophronia moved on, though, John still had the shoes and that bothered Manny.

John took to the business.

It ain't for everybody trying to know things you don't.

John, though, took to it. A lot of new guys come in for their day's training and the next day you see where they got their act from; a little of Tractor's plowing through, some of Ben's bullshit word play, and always, I think, too much of me. John, though, had us all stealing from him after a week. Smooooooth. Jean Bratón he called himself.

"Yes, ma'am," he'd say, "if we might sit quietly for a few minutes," and he'd pause, "if we might sit quietly I shall begin to channel my gifts through you toward your necklace, and then, and this, ma'am, is only through the utmost effort on both of our parts, through quiet, focused channeling, we will begin to bring our gifts home, back through you, and to me, hoping, focusing as well, ma'am, because hope alone as you know is not enough or you would already have your necklace back, for I can see you during all those times of hope and worry which washed over you like the great rains of the Testaments. Are you ready then, ma'am, for us to sit together in this sincere fashion?"

Never seen them say no. Not once. Well, one time I was home watching a movie and Tractor called me, couldn't believe it, said, "Somebody turned down Jean Bratón."

"Fuck you," I heard John say in the background.

Every other time, though, when he'd get them settled down, he'd put down the phone, leave them sitting there channeling and focusing, and he'd go outside for a cigarette.

Wasn't long John started talking about going into the business himself, which would have been fine except Tractor, he started this business, pointed out fine print that should have been in the contract about that sort of thing.

"Means what you've learned and developed, etc., etc., in the psychic phone business belongs to the United States Psychic Alliance."

Things were never quite the same between those two from then on.

Wasn't a week after that, though, I hear John over there, got some fellow going along, asking about his love life and that sort of thing, and he says, "Sir, and this is something I'd only recommend in a case such as yours, but sir, what I see for you in today's world of sexual disease and perversion, the safest, most healthy sex life for your future involves something in which you've already placed great trust and that is, of course, sir, the telephone. Yes sir, let me get you this number of a business Jean Bratón recommends highly: Sophronia's Phone Funhouse."

Despite all the psychics around here, as of yet nobody's been willing to speculate out loud how John's wife actually come to meet Manny the Cobbler face to face, but there's no denying it was John first sent him her way.

It's hard to get in more than a "Your special he or she is going to come to his or her as-of-late misguided senses and come back to you" with him in the background. And he won't listen to a thing I say on the matter so I decide, hell with it, I'll by god call Tractor.

"I'll kill the bastard," Tractor said.

When I told John he got the biggest see-I'm-psychic, told-you-so grin and said, "Since I am going it'd sure be funny to leave Tractor a little trouble on my way out."

And so now I got to try to make my couple of dollars with him beside me working the other side of things, and me knowing any minute Tractor's going to bust in and all John's going to have for him's that grin.

That's when I get my idea.

Now at no time did I think the idea was good, but my approach, following an idea out like that, can bring me across another idea, one I might call good. Probably that's what I was hoping for out of calling Sophronia.

I knew I'd have to approach her careful, but not as to sound careful. Clear, but not like I had to be clear for her. More like I'd talk to her if she'd called me, something she'd never done, not directly, though I'm sure she did, in fact, call me a few things indirectly back when me and John first learned about Teddy's.

Teddy's was two blocks from where we worked and the second closest place we could get a drink. It cost five dollars to get in, but they had food, though it was little food, and, well, they had their waitresses wearing teddies.

John had told Sophronia Teddy's was a sports bar named after some forward on the old New York Nets.

"Who ever heard of anybody on the Nets but Dr. J?" I asked him.

"Exactly," he said.

When she found out different she didn't have to say a word to any of us at work, you could read her mind in her step, in the way she picked up her feet between steps.

Something about the way she said hello on the phone sounded the same as when she'd walk, that same clip.

Surprised hell out of me when she said yes, she'd come down and talk with John about this dying mess.

But before we got off the phone she said she had this little story she wanted to tell me. She'd always wanted to tell me.

Her mother'd been widowed at nineteen, Viet Nam and all, and little Sophronia was already three, still remembers them getting the call, and she and her mother in that way, as she put it, grew up together.

"When you were telling me about John I realized my mama, of all the people in the world, had it right. Ain't that a damn thing?"

"One time," she said, "this man, Mr. Putney, who worked on our car, gave Mama this bird." I was sitting there watching John on the phone giving away money, listening to his ex-wife tell me a bird story, and waiting on Tractor to come in any minute and turn the whole place into a red-faced, fat-grabbing wrestling match.

"Mama wasn't going to put anything in a cage," she was saying, "so she just let the bird around the house. Liked to get in drawers and things. Liked to drink out of your glass. Anyway, a couple years later, Mama got a boyfriend, and something about her bird hopping around made that fellow, Sid Burns, not think highly of her. He'd call her names. Then for Christmas got her a birdcage. Got drunk that night and threw it at her. On New Year's Day, though, she shot him in the back of the head. Did four and a half years and on the day she got out we sat drinking margaritas and she said, 'If you do for a man, generally they'll do for you. If they don't do for you, you just do them in.'"

"You say John believes he's reached the day his sun's to set?" she asked me. "I wouldn't miss it for the world, not the whole world."

When she hung up I heard the Corvette pulling up outside and shot John the "Here comes Tractor" look, but he didn't break stride. In fact he grinned, telling somebody, "So spread the word, the answer's in our heart, not in our hand."

When Tractor walked in he took the phone from John, pinching himself between the eyes, and said, with the best enunciation I've heard in a while, "John, tell me what in hell you are doing."

"My best," John said.

"What's that?"

"Doing my best is all."

Tractor twisted a little between his eyes, which were shut tighter than I'd have guessed possible.

Both phones were ringing.

Tractor, and I know it's because he couldn't think straight about John, I knew it then, looked at me, talking about, "You dying, too, or you still working around here?"

So I answered the phone. And because neither Tractor nor John knew what they wanted to say next, they both turned their attention to me. And this fellow's on the other end saying, "Wife tells me her psychic called and turned on her."

"Sir, what can I do for you?" I asked him, getting out my good pen and pad, using my roman numerals.

"Want to know what you expect me to do with these bills."

"Sir, I'm not sure what you mean." I did scratch through my roman numeral I.

"You don't expect us to pay now?"

I didn't need this. Tractor didn't. John didn't. Not then. We were all there, not needing this.

Then Sophronia walked in and did that thing where she flashes the light switch twice.

Said right off, "Always knew you'd make a big scene about going, John."

She'd dressed for the occasion. Not quite widow black, though. More what people wear to slip from dinner to late night. With the boots.

"We smoke outside," Tractor told her.

"I'm sorry, Tractor, and how are you?"

She put her cigarette out in a cup I guess John was through drinking from.

"Look, this ain't no social situation," Tractor started. "Your husband there ..."

"Ex," she said.

"Ex, then, has lost his damn mind."

"Well, my mama always said you got to have something before you can lose it."

"That's an expression." It was the fellow on the other end of the line.

"Yes, sir," I said.

"Well?" he asked me.

"What?" I asked him.

"Tell them."

"Tell them what?"

"Tell them it's just an expression, losing your mind is."

"Sir, you realize this is costing you money?"

"That's what I called about. Course if it's to cost me, seems like you'd tell them what I said."

"He says losing your mind's an expression."

"Who?" they all asked.

"Him," I said, shaking the phone.

"Is he paying?" Tractor asked.

And John got up, stretched real big, and said, "It is endearing to have those close to me gathered tonight."

Sophronia took out her lipstick and mirror and started in on herself.

Tractor started what we used to call his plowing, stringing together cuss words with no distinctions between them so, if you were to write down what Tractor was saying, it'd look like one big word and would sound like a different language if you were to try to read what you'd written.

Sophronia was making this sort of smacking noise and kissing a napkin, then putting a little lipstick back on, smacking and kissing the napkin again.

"What in the world?" the fellow on the phone wanted to know.

I didn't know what to tell him.

All I knew was Tractor was going to bust at any juncture. The only thing, I believe, that had saved John so far from an old-fashioned ass-whupping was his rubbery attitude, the way he was holding himself, or really, wasn't holding himself, like he had really given himself over.

"He's getting pretty worked up." It was the fellow on the phone again.

"Yeah," I said because, well, he was.

"What's going to happen?" he asked me.

"How in hell should I know?" I asked him, and Tractor quit cussing and Sophronia quit with the lipstick. John got this proud look over him.

The fellow on the other end started telling his wife, way off in the distance, how the guy on the phone, me, "ain't no more psychic than you, Doris," and John was aiming his voice over at the telephone, "Sir, that's what I been trying to tell you," when all of the sudden there's this horn blowing out in the parking lot, almost like one of those alarms, but more persistent.

Tractor reared up in a fury and rolled out the door. Made the calendar fall off the wall.

"I was wondering when he'd show up," John said, and we were all scared to know who he meant, but it wasn't hard to figure out. Tractor came right back in. Said to Sophronia, "Good thing you're warmed up." She was still kissing the napkin, though she'd about run out of fresh places.

Tractor was looking more at John until the honking started back, and he turned to her and said, "Well, go settle things down with him."

"Who?" Sophronia asked.

"Manny the damn Cobbler."

"I'm not going out there. I quit him."

"Well, he ain't quit you."

"I'll go out there," John said, and even with one of the phones ringing, and Manny the Cobbler's honking, a silence came over the room like a sickness. It was a well-known fact Manny the Cobbler had once served time. For bad checks.

"Just remember," Tractor told him, "he learned things any ordinary man on the street don't know how to defend."

"That ain't all he learned," Sophronia smacked.

"I'm going," John said, jumping to his feet. "Told y'all this was coming."

And we let him go.

And when the door closed, the room felt like a parallelogram, and the man on the line, his wife was yelling at him now how it was costing money and all, but all he wanted to know was should he call 911.

Tractor and Sophronia looked like they were listening for their names, leaning forward, their hands on their knees.

"Well, should I call them?" the fellow wanted to know.

"Just be quiet a minute," I told him.

"I can't," he said.

I asked him why.

"The wife. It's costing us money."

"Here," I told him, "I'll call you right back."

Tractor loved that.

But the guy's wife picks up the phone asking if this was some kind of game show or anything to be aware of.

"Ma'am, my friend might be out there getting killed," I told her. "That sound like a game to you?"

"Well, let me give you back over to my husband."

"What in the hell?" Tractor asked me.

"First, I want to ask you something." It was the man's wife.

"Ma'am," I said.

And I couldn't tell if she said her and her husband were out in the country or out of the country because John walked in saying how he'd made peace with Manny, didn't call him Manny the Cobbler.

"Ain't that bad a guy," John said.

Manny barely beeped a couple of polite beeps in the background.

"Why don't you go out and talk to him?" John asked Sophronia, who smirked but not much. "Make him feel better about everything? I've got to get back to work."

CIRO, SEDUCER OF MAIDS

Juanita believes Ciro looked at her through a window, though it seems impossible he'd be within spitting distance when you see our sign. It looks more like the back of a sign, the part you're not supposed to see, not the flower which attracts the bee.

You've worked hard, Patrice, but flowers pasted on wood are not neon. Only neon flowing through the letters of Las Bonitas will bring Ciro to us.

There is the man who sells neon, but his price is too high for maids and Boss says neon does nothing for a traveler. Clean your rooms, he says, and does that thing with his eyes that makes me think of the rings around Saturn but is supposed to mean get back to work.

Juanita believes Ciro looked at her, but the glare on our glass is strong and Ciro's eyes have surely weakened by now. And there is the matter of his reflection, for, as Juanita would say, to see Ciro is to know a picture worth a thousand words is worth nothing. Ciro, seducer of maids, is like the raindrop out there which never hits ground. Some believe it will fall soon. Some do not believe anything. And there are those—Patrice, Juanita—who thirst and, should the rings of Saturn loosen, would drink the raindrop down.

There are tales at market of how Ciro stayed at a motel as long as three days. The maids of that motel now have faces like the moon behind fast moving clouds. It's hard not to hate them at market, their arms never so full they can't snicker and tell stories of his snoring.

We wring beddings from our breast. Somewhere women have hands in dough, and there are women who become president, but we work in waiting, weaving these tales. We know what's out there hanging from a cloud.

Our husbands and lovers, fathers and brothers, are beautiful, but Ciro keeps them sacred, so we tattoo our left breast for him, our right for the others.

Juanita's husband has beat her. Though he is beautiful his weakness wraps him in the rings of Saturn. What is he going to do?

One day forget to finish crossing the street and become part of a taxi cab.

Juanita did not tell her husband of Ciro, but her eyes moved.

When we are little and dream of carnivals and animals and sometimes monsters we are always brought back to this world of corners. Awake. But Ciro leaves us in the swerves between. You can see it in the way Juanita's eyes move.

This is why the tradition of needles must be honored.

Because once Maria was found in one of her rooms with little line between dream and death and no memory of the jeweled ceiling or wine-stained walls, the fruit peels filling the bathtub, or roses and chocolate in the trash can. So we sew needles in the hems of these sheets and hold them between our fingers with Ciro between our legs, the pain of one piercing balancing the pleasure of the other.

And because we are looking after she who is next, we sew with the next needle we hide.

The man who sells neon uses words like barter and business, but he wants sex.

I showed him our sign, cracked and brittle, and he scratched out his smile, said neon will bring back suppleness.

I have heard sex with him is not as bad as one might think. And I have heard the same thing about being stretched between two horses over fire.

If you ride from the city, the signs are not brittle, and the colors play upon your face and you know we need neon.

We are picked clean of flowers.

Patrice is plainly beautiful perched on our sign with paint and weeds, but I have had it with plain and paint.

Tonight I will invite the man who sells neon into one of my rooms. Soon if you ride from the city you will see no sign greater than ours.

Patrice, I forbid you to climb. We will have neon now. Brush your hair.

A wish from a maid is like shit from a horse.

This is what the man who sells neon told me when my eyes moved.

This is why the rings will tighten on him after I do.

And why I give you my rooms. One day you will be me.

And young girls who will gather in the glow of our great sign will tuck their hair behind their ears to hear the beginning of his name far off somewhere, maybe from the place where wind begins. They will put Patrice's old painted weeds on a stick and raise it above them in the air, and tell my story like they're at market.

THE BRIDGE

This all started when I went and showed Tammi where I wrote her name on the bridge going over the new highway.

That's when she told me, on the way over there. The next day I bought a brand new hawkbill knife from Mr. Dwight's store.

She said it was either me or her uncle.

She said, "Nathan, it *feels* like your baby."

That made me feel better, but I had this thing spinning around in my head like a lawn mower about how many times she'd done it with him and when and who else knew and where and all. I even asked her sitting there on the bridge, watching the cars go underneath, how come she kept doing it with him if she didn't like it. She didn't say nothing for a while and then it was something about how she couldn't believe I could write her name so good upside down hanging off the bridge. I told her I didn't really like the way the 'a' turned out, though Bo Morris told me he thought it looked good driving through, which was another good thing, the fact that there wasn't a chance that the baby inside Tammi belonged to Bo Morris. He was my best friend and I would have hated to have to kill him over all this.

Tammi's uncle had some long foreign name or something so everybody just called him C. L. When I was little I'd go by his trailer and look at the rattlesnake he kept in a cage made out of chickenwire. That snake was big then. His name was Tex.

C. L. was the meanest man in Roberdel. Bo Morris told me if C.L. ever caught you looking at that snake he'd make you hold him. Nobody, not even C. L., wanted to hold Tex.

See, that's just it. I figured C. L. was sleeping with Tammi out of the only reason he done anything—pure meanness. I mean his wife was pretty. She was Tammi's mama's sister, and all the women in that family are pretty. The kind of pretty that makes decisions for a man.

It's kind of hard to tell how much older C. L. was than Tammi because C. L. was one of those you couldn't really tell how old he was. Tammi was 13. Now I will admit she didn't look 13 at the time. I mean I was 18 then and I never felt embarrassed with her like at the shopping center or nothing. I loved her. I wanted to get Bo Morris to tattoo her name on my arm with Indian ink, but my daddy, he's got tattoos all over him, told me once when I'd just wrote her name on my arm with a regular old pen that if I ever got one he'd cut it out of me. There's a list of names on my daddy's right arm and each one has a line tattooed through it in the same color ink as the next name. My mama's name ain't even on there because she wouldn't have it on there with them other women and told Daddy she'd do what he said he'd do to me if he did put her name on there, so there's a line through the last name, without a matching color name under it. Daddy told me Mama still has to see them names everyday. Anyway, that's why I wrote her name on the bridge. I figured everybody'd know who wrote it. When I wrote it I said to myself how there wouldn't ever be no line through this name. I had plenty of other things to worry about. Like killing C. L. Covington. See, I'd already made my decision when I bought that knife and all. I'm just that way. I make a decision and stick to it.

Like when I stole Coach Campbell's car. I'd planned on leaving school, stealing the coach's car and going for a ride and being back by Gym so he wouldn't be able to say I did it. Somebody told on me or something because he didn't even drive his car that day, so I walked all the way to his house and stole his damn car anyway and drove it to school like I hadn't even done nothing, and that night the police come, but didn't much happen to me because I was only 14 and Mama cried so much. All that started because he stopped letting me wear jeans in PE.

See, that's just why I went and bought that knife—so I'd have to do it, kill C. L. I mean I got knives and all. Most of them better than that cheap hawkbill I bought from Mr. Dwight. But buying that knife, that was me making a deal with myself. You buy this knife, you kill C. L. That's what I was saying to myself.

So there I was walking around with it in my pocket and a hawkbill knife's no good for throwing at trees or nothing which I reckon that's why I got it because like I said that knife was part of a deal. And it would be there reminding me of my half of the bargain, like it was saying, "You done gone and bought me, Nathan Hunt, now use me."

It wasn't new to Tammi for me to be carrying a knife and she don't know a hawkbill from a switchblade so she never really asked me much about it or nothing. And she never much brought up C. L. I figured maybe she thought I was scared of him. She didn't even talk about the baby, I mean what she was going to do. We mainly'd just walk around, maybe go sit on the bridge and pick out cars that we'd have one day and sometimes she'd ask me, "Nathan, if you knew it was your baby, we'd raise it together, and give it a good home and everything, right?"

And I'd look back at her and tell her how if I knew it was mine, if I knew it was, I'd take a job, any shift, hell, double shift, and I'd take care of both her and the baby. And she'd look at me like I broke her heart, but I don't know what she really expected me to say. I mean I wasn't going to raise no kid of C. L. Covington's. So every time she'd ask me something like that and then get all crying-eyed, that hawkbill'd be there. Just reminding me.

Now this was supposed to be my senior year, but I wasn't really counting on graduating because my English teacher didn't like me. In our school if you don't pass English you don't pass the grade and I had this problem every year, except this one was worse on account of Mrs. Rollings not liking me. See, ever since ninth grade I'd spent most of my schooling in the trade shops learning welding and body work, but they still want you to pass that English. I feel like I speak English as good as any welder ever needs to. I mean I feel like I can tell you something every bit as good as Mrs. Rollings, but she don't know the first thing about striking an arc. What really don't make sense to me is, say I was going to teach Mrs. Rollings some simple spot welding, what language would I use to teach her with? See, I know enough of the one to teach her the other and she don't know nothing except about the one. And she's the teacher. She was all the time wanting to tell me how I got potential and all until one day I told her, in class, that I'm sure she had lots of welding potential.

That's all my mama ever asked me, to get that diploma, and if it wasn't Mrs. Rollings or Coach trying to keep me from it, it was somebody like C. L. keeping my mind off it. I was going to take care of C. L. and, well, you can't kill a school teacher except I really did almost want to kill Coach that once when I took his car, but he's cleared in my mind because we made a deal and I don't have to take PE no more.

Nothing would ever clear C. L. in my mind unless Tammi was just to come out and say she made the whole thing up, but Tammi ain't that kind of girl. The days were going by and that knife was getting bigger in my pocket just like Tammi said her belly was, but I couldn't tell about that. She'd get me to put my ear on her belly and I'd lie and say, "Dammit, Tammi Miller, it sounds like a big old Hunt baby."

It didn't sound any different than how it used to when I'd lay my head on her at the ball park. Just a bunch of shook noises.

She'd asked me could she tell her mama, when she did tell her, that it was my baby because she didn't think it'd be right to tell her she was pregnant *and* about how it might be C. L. at the same time. That was fine with me. I didn't want anybody to know about her and C. L. if I could help it. I figured one day soon wouldn't nobody know about it at all except me and Tammi and I could forget about it little by little with him gone until it wasn't nothing. Nothing but something somebody could have dreamed, or seen on TV. Or even just plain old nothing.

Then that Friday morning I got up to breakfast smell before Mama come in my room. She was still cleaning up Daddy's dishes. I remember she offered to make me a breakfast, but I didn't see any reason at the time to have anything besides my cereal. I watched the news with Mama and I wanted to ask her about them names on Daddy's arms. We'd always pretended like, around one another, them names wasn't even there. I wanted to ask her did it still hurt.

And other things. You can't ask your mama about things like that, though. She offered to drop me off at school on the way to the mill, but I told her how I was meeting Bo, and how we still had pep rallies on Fridays and so it didn't matter if I was late. We'd been through that before and she'd said, "Long as you don't miss what you're there for."

What she meant was, well, she didn't think I was going to school to cheer the football team any more than I did.

"You be there for your studies, though. Make sure you're ready for the Lord's plan."

That's what she said to me on her way out. It's kind of stuck with me. See, I'd given up on the Lord having any plan for me. I mean I'm sure he has a plan for some folks, like preachers and all, but I'd decided that I was one of them folks he just wasn't sure what to do with. It didn't really bother me too much. Wasn't my fault. The way I saw it, it was plenty of us. I mean you can't tell me it's God's plan for Mama to work at Klopman all her life or Daddy at the chicken plant. If that's it, then well, it ain't a good one. I'd decided a long time ago, before I ever quit Sunday school even, that if that's what the Lord had planned for me he could just forget it. I make my own plans.

On the way there to meet Bo at the bridge I thought about Tammi's name on it. I could remember this one time when they first built it. We was there, me and Tammi and some other people, but it was before we were going together or anything. She was young then. She was young, but she owned that bridge. Every time I ever held her, it felt just like how she looked then.

Now I wondered did C. L. drive through and laugh at me and maybe tell his friends. I figured he did. I figured he got a kick out of it and I touched that hawkbill. Just then the schoolbus I used to ride went by and somebody hollered 'redneck' at me and I didn't even bother trying to figure out who it was. I was too busy with my plan. My own plan. See, I knew C. L. worked second shift and Tammi'd told me he slept until noon and how he was even meaner then. I was going to be there when he woke up.

When I got to the bridge Bo was already dropping little pebbles off when cars went by.

"Ain't big enough to hurt anybody, just crack some windshields," he told me.

Folks were slamming on their brakes, but they couldn't turn around or nothing and Bo, he'd just shoot them the bird. Maybe that was the Lord's plan for Bo. Maybe he'd always be shooting BBs at people coming out of the store. See, I wanted to talk to Bo about what I wanted to do and all, but I didn't want to tell him why. I don't know, I just didn't want him thinking that way about her.

"Bo, I need to talk to you. Just you and me, okay?" I had that hawkbill out and didn't even know it. Bo did, though.

"Let me see."

"Listen to me," I said, handing him the knife. "I got something to take care of and I'm going to kind of need your help."

"You got this from Mr. Dwight?" He was seeing how sharp it was, and all the things you do to check a knife.

"Dammit, Bo, just give me the thing. I need to talk to you," and he just stood there looking at me like he couldn't just say okay or nothing now because I didn't want to talk about the knife. "I want to talk to you about something, but not too much, okay?"

He didn't say nothing. Like it was the worst thing in the world, me not wanting to talk about that knife. Anyway, I just come right out and told him,

"Bo, I aim to kill C. L." Now you got to understand, at that time, C. L. was like a legend or something to Bo, like Rambo or somebody, I don't know, but if you'd seen his face you'd know what I mean. Bo got up and started walking around and then, just in case, I reckon, he asked me, "What?" and I told him just what I'd already said, that I was going to kill C. L. One thing about Bo, he always wants to know the how more than he does the why.

"With that hawkbill, Nathan? You going to kill C. L. with a pocket knife? He's got more guns than ... man, he's got them bullets that'll kill you if they hit you in the foot."

"That's what I want to talk to you about."

"How am I going to talk to you about that? About getting yourself all blown to hell? Why you want to go messing with that devil?"

See, that's what I didn't want to talk to him about.

And didn't neither one of us say something for a long time. Bo picked up a rock, a rock like a baseball, and this big eighteen-wheeler was coming carrying new cars and I was scared what he was going to do, but I didn't stop him or nothing. And he threw it, not at the cab or nothing, but just creamed one of them new, I believe it was, Plymouths.

The driver didn't even notice.

"Good shot," I told him and for a little while it was like we were back in the days we used to have, and I remember there was diesel in the air.

"I don't want to go to jail, Bo," I told him after a while.

"You going to be lucky if you go to jail."

"All the same, I don't want to go. I mean I don't want to get killed or nothing either," and we didn't neither one say nothing, and then I said, "I need you to help me plan this out without asking a whole bunch of questions."

"Plan how to kill C. L.?"

"Yeah."

And these next few things Bo tried to come up with'll show you how good a friend he can be.

"What if we spray-paint his trailer?"

"No."

"How about we sugar the gas tank of that new Jeep?"

"Uh-uh, Bo."

"I got it, Nathan," he said. "We'll kill Tex. That's it, that'll get him, we'll sneak up there while he's sleeping and kill that son-of-a-bitch snake."

See, Bo was willing to jump right in, scared as he was of C. L. and of that snake, and do any of them things just to try and save me. I let him down, though.

"I got to kill him, Bo."

Now Bo, he had a moped he'd taken things off and put other things on so it would look as little like a moped as he could get it. It'd go pretty good and we took the thing and headed toward C. L.'s. See, my plan wasn't all that fancy or anything, but I figured Bo, he'd knock on the door and I'd be out by Tex, and Bo, he'd tell C. L. how I wasn't scared of him and why don't he come make me hold Tex. That's when I planned on killing him, right when he was getting the snake out. Bo said how that sounded like a good plan except why don't I go to the door.

I asked him, "Bo, you really think C. L.'s going to believe you want to hold that Tex?" Bo didn't like thinking about Tex.

Now it's a pretty good ride over to where C. L. lives, but it didn't seem like no time because how I was thinking about Tammi and me and different times we had together and how, once all this was over with, I'd be glad she told me. Meant I could trust her.

When we got there I went on over by Tex and was looking at him and everything. He was demons and devils and C. L. and my daddy when he's drunk, all stuffed and sewed up in a snake skin. He was laying there like he wasn't even in a cage at all and he was a fat snake. A snake don't look sloppy fat like people do. They carry their fat like clothes. Bo said how C. L wouldn't hardly feed him or nothing just to keep him mean and that sometimes he'd use a stick and let him out on a dog or something. Looked fed. He was laying there like they do—so still it put movement in the air around him.

I asked Bo was he ready to knock on the door.

"Hell no, I ain't ready, Nathan. Do I look ready to get involved in this—sit here and watch you get beat to death?"

"Bo," I told him, "I need you to go and knock on the door."

"He's going to be mad."

"Good. I'm going to get mad with him."

"Nathan, let's just kill Tex." He knew what that answer was.

Bo, he took his time going to the door, but he went. He knocked the kind of knock you don't want anybody to hear and he looked at me. I wasn't scared at the time, I was doing it for me and Tammi and the baby, but I felt sorry for Bo. He didn't want anybody coming to that door, but they did and they opened it ever so careful and I could tell, looking at Bo standing there looking in, and then at me, and then in again, that it wasn't C. L., it wasn't C. L. at all. The way he was piecing things together he figured out why we was there about the same time I figured out who was at the door. I could tell he was hurting. And then it just occurred to me about Tex. I opened his cage, I swear to God, and I pulled him out like he wasn't mean old Tex at all and he kind of hung there lazy-like against my leg. He was heavy, but he wasn't slimy or nothing and he wasn't fat, it was muscle. Things were in slow motion so I couldn't make out what Tammi and Bo was yelling. I could hear her, but I never saw her. I took Tex over by the woods and I let him go. I don't know why he didn't bite me, maybe because it was so hot. Bo said he knew I was going to let him go and all. C. L. never come out.

Many times as I had to go through that bridge I didn't draw a line through Tammi's name. I wasn't starting a list.

FOOTPRAYER

There's the old prayer for the feet, having to do with the connection to Earth and others through that grounding, the connection to all who've gone before, the ashes-to-ashes, dust-to-dust thing.

One step, two step, old step, new step.

There's the old smell of water and fresh dirt. A long time ago you watched a bird fly the whole sky, you waded in the lake and let little schools of small fish brush your legs. You listened to the cats calling out your window to nobody at all.

Then a cow with her calf came up in your back yard and you never told anyone.

You fell down in rain and stood up in lightning and somewhere the whole scene still flashes silver, the clouds cut past the glare of the rain, and the shine shapes a spire while water falls from the center of the sky into the glow of it all.

Makes the meaning go away. Even in a story.

But maybe it'll mean something this time.

Or maybe all you see are words. It's not even real.

That's the thing. This story'll sit here, untold. Like when you're riding other pages.

But you want this story to mean something, or will. You will want that. When somebody's reading or listening, more than anything you want meaning in the mean old world.

Fine.

You might believe your story says something about you. Okay, but this story's forgotten over and over, like memories of what you wish you hadn't done.

So this story's never told and nothing ever happens instead.

You and the other runners gathered, stretched quietly, took places, and at the sound of the shot burst out of your stances. Together and in the first few steps you still felt part of everything.

But like any other example from time, the second hand passing the minute, the minute the hour, you got left behind.

And with a long way to go.

And the rain, different shines showing up in the water.

And cheers for the winner, and increasingly fewer cheers for the rest, intent to their last step, overrunning the line, leaning into their stop, hands on their knees, looking up for a water bottle from an anonymous hand.

You ran alongside windmilling arms.

When you first fell, you struggled straight to your feet and for a few steps ran the way you did once in your front yard, the same sun somewhere in the sky.

Then, losing yourself, morphing into a set of flailing knees and elbows, your head's heaviness pulled you face first into a short-stubbed, knee-locked step that took you off track into the middle of everything. The weight of your head snatched you this way then that, then finally back, somehow, into the appropriate lane, where your sudden singing startled the crowd.

Kids walked up to their parents or somebody else's parents and leaned against their sides and waited out your prayer-scat.

Maybe it means something for a change. It's a lot to ask for you to finish. You've run this race forever and you don't always get this far.

STRUGGLE DANCING

On Mayday, what would have been her grandmother's ninetieth birthday, Ann-Mrie Hunt left Beaumont in a baby blue, four-door Falcon that had been sitting in the front yard on four flat tires for four years since her grandmother died falling off the front porch.

Ann-Mrie said to her mother, "I'm going to take a job on that riverboat casino in Lake Charles." And even though her mother would've said the f-word if it might not make her fall off the very same porch, and even though her daddy quit fixing the window broken after a softball game to say the Falcon wouldn't make it but the one way, Ann-Mrie bought new tires. She wanted to ride out of town on the same gas her grandmother had put in. Her daddy said it was half water. She said she thought all gas was half water.

When Ann-Mrie left Beaumont her favorite radio station was playing "One of These Nights." She turned it up. Then she turned it back down. And then off, speeding up a little. That sort of song would not be her favorite anymore.

At the consignment shop, where the week before she had taken any clothes she would not be needing at a casino, they gave her thirty-seven dollars and told her how a cheerleader type had bought everything but the yellow dress, which they offered her eight dollars for. She took it.

Ann-Mrie drove by the cemetery on her way out of town. She could hear her grandmother as if she'd never been in the ground, her torn-linen voice saying, "There's a certain pulling at a person," the same words she'd spoken just before she fell off the porch, when Ann-Mrie came running out in the dress that matched her grandmother's except for how it had faded in the sun.

And then that sudden, spreading, red-edged spot just at the neckline.

Coroner said he wouldn't bury her in such a thin, thready dress, so at the funeral Ann-Mrie lay across her grandmother, across the black and the yellow, put a daisy below her chin, and thought for the first time about the Lake Charles Riverboat Casino.

Johnson McCrae had a good life. Had been a pit boss in Reno for four and a half years. Before that he'd dealt blackjack in Vegas at the Riviera. Before that had pitched double-A baseball, and before that been in love with a girl named Cindy.

Had not been in love since. Wasn't going to be. Had a good life.

A man like Johnson McCrae did not need but one time where the place in between asleep and awake is full of pictures you can't see, where there is that line pulling you from your center, where the sun is something you bounce in your hand.

The more he held it, though, like ice, the more it would change. The tighter he'd try to hold on, the smaller it would become, eventually running right through his fingers.

Wasn't going to be in love again. Had a good life now.

Thing was, Ann-Mrie Hunt was bearing down on the Lake Charles Riverboat Casino, her eyes her headlights, pulled along by the telephone lines, thicker, tighter even, than the prettiest black snakes, and she was pulled by the big royal trucks that sometimes run over snakes and leave them there popping at the world, in the sun, in the rain, in places only those that move after death know about.

Out there in between.

And she was thinking about that yellow dress.

That, and about the day in Beaumont when the sun had been

the brightest it had ever been. Everybody'd said so. Said outright how if anything had happened that day it would have been too hard to notice and harder still to remember because of the silver sun, the dime stuck in its belly, sucking up shade.

The streets pulled themselves in that day.

No one could hold an expression.

Birds couldn't get more than three feet off the ground before the sun, heavy on the tops of cars, pressing in their shade, beat them down.

Somebody'd be getting that dress that could use it.

Johnson McCrae could not see what his painting had to do with any moon. And in fact, if he ever named them at all, it was after the work was done, when the only way out of the corner of his head he was always painting himself into was to call it something.

The painting was bright, nothing fading. And no moon.

No moon at all but that title, "Fading Moon," its letters bright, the word 'Fading' bright as the top of water, hanging in the air just above the canvas as he worked.

When Johnson McCrae left Reno he gave his latest painting to a call girl from Phoenix who said she liked it, would hang it on her wall, and that, if he would sign it, she would remember his name forever.

She had started not to charge him that night, but they could neither one go through with it. She needed the money and he had it.

That breath of paint, barely even on the canvas, could have been called "Fading Moon," but that had not occurred to him.

And here was this painting taking the name down upon itself in spite of its whipping-sharp shine.

There was just no need for a dress like that at a casino where everything, she had seen in movies, was roulette red and roulette black. Red and black. The suits of the men and the suits of the cards. Red dog. Blackjack.

Never yellow.

The lines on the road were suddenly all she had, and even they were not always there, and not really that yellow at all.

His paints were still out. He had forty-five minutes until he'd have to leave for work, and his paints were still out, ready to put in the last, the lasting, to make the picture move.

A few times he'd picked up his brush, reached towards a particular paint, a particular color, and then withdrawn, putting his brush back down.

He had thirty minutes now.

He turned on CNN. Went and looked at the painting. Maybe it was done, maybe could do without anything else. Keep it understated, subtle.

But the painting would not let go like that. Something could keep the thing from just sitting there, and the painting itself seemed to know.

He looked through his mail.

Ten minutes now. Five.

In the shine of the painting, not too far but a little down into it, down in the shine, he could barely see some turn, some stirring, suggestion, swerve, but how to pull it out, bring it to surface, to light?

It was time to go.

And the painting showed him.

He took up the brush, twisting it thick in color, touching just the spot suggested, and pulled a thickening line out from the very heart of the painting, letting it end in its own exploding eruption. Yellow.

The boy at the gas station had rags in all his pockets. "One for your windows, one for your oil, and one for my hands," he'd said, and when she didn't ask, "Usually say the other'n's for my back-up. Either that or I say it's for the customer, I mean if you need it."

He'd done a cartwheel for her when she'd taken it and pulled off, and he started jumping up and down and flapping his arms, a rag in each hand, keeping at it for as long as she looked in the trembling rear-view, letting her new rag flap in her hand like a flag on a float in a parade.

The radio was doing its best, offering up all sorts of songs, some sort of familiar, some as strange to her as deep snow. She sang at some.

Then a woman telling everybody in radio land about a big sale at some furniture store sounded like Ann-Mrie Hunt's tenth-grade math teacher, Mrs. Spivey, who drove a car her husband had built out of a kit he'd ordered from a magazine, when she'd say how much something was, something about how she put her numbers.

The kind of thing Mrs. Spivey might say is, "That dress is worth more'n any eight dollars, Ann-Mrie. Easy."

"Hello, Mr. McCrae," they'd say, or just, "Mr. McCrae," with a little nod, and he always tried to speak back, remembered what it was like to try and make your mark, stand out in a place where the most important thing is that you don't.

He hurried through the buffet, putting together a salad, knowing no matter how much he wanted to do something different with it, when he sat down in his office it would look the same as yesterday's. And, even so, somebody, usually a tip-charged waitress, would just have to say before he could get there, "Sure is a good-looking salad, Mr. McCrae."

He liked sunflower seeds where he used to like bacon bits.

In his office were four television screens, built into the wall, three always showing changing angles of the tables. The fourth was regular TV, hooked up to the satellite that sat atop the captain's quarters, bouncing beams of soft porn and sports of the fringe, such as tractor pulls, into his office.

But all he watched on it was *The Andy Griffith Show*. "The finest show on television" came on three times during his shift, and he worked around them.

The rest of the time if he was in his office he was watching the other three screens, without the black and white indifference he had to wear out there, watching not so much for cheaters and thieves, he could spot them without looking, but for the drama of a woman playing with her salary, or a man playing with somebody else's.

Anytime Ann-Mrie Hunt smelled garbage burning she'd think of barbecue. And she'd think of when she and her grandmother would go for their rides in the country, smelling barbecue smoldering in the smoking leaves and trash piled in the squared-off yards of the grown children of whoever owned this ranch or that farm.

She remembered once on one of those rides they'd come up on a dog sleeping in the road.

And Ann-Mrie'd thought it had been hit by a car, but her grandmother'd said how it just looked too comfortable to have been hit by a car, and they sat there looking at that dog until Ann-Mrie said if he hadn't been hit by a car now he might be soon, laying there like that, and could she pet him.

Her grandmother said no, he might have something you could catch, and their car pulled off, Ann-Mrie saying she could get a stick.

And though Ann-Mrie knew it wasn't the same day, in the movie her memory was showing, she and her grandmother went and had barbecue somewhere, and she drank her Coke out of the bottle, dreaming of having a yellow dress like her grandmother's, one with that yellow that announces itself, even in church. Says me and this person I'm on are here. We have our own way, can walk just as fast as we like.

We don't have to go in when it's raining.

Got sun in pocket.

Talked at by a drunk parts salesman from Mississippi who'd run off most of the table, Johnson McCrae watched how his new dealer, a woman born in Africa, handled him. And he did his smile.

"She's a good'n," the man said, splitting aces. "Where'd you find her? England?"

Johnson McCrae did his smile.

A queen and an eight. To her seventeen.

"Hot a mighty, I'm telling you, boss, I'm going to follow her around tonight, make enough money off her she'll have to marry me."

Johnson McCrae made a note that his dealer wasn't easily shaken.

"Where's my waitress?"

Johnson McCrae did his smile.

"Tell my waitress I want my usual." The man, shaking ice out of his glass, said, "She don't know what my usual is, boss, you ask her why."

But Johnson did his smile.

His waitress, a woman from Houston with sky features, brought him his drink. He didn't tip.

"Look over there, boss," he said, "that big fat son-bitch. Man I work for in Jackson's fatter than that. Son-bitch. Somebody's got to help him go to the bathroom." The man thought about it a while and said, "Son-bitch."

Johnson McCrae did his best.

Ann-Mrie Hunt's road was above water before she knew it, telephone lines hiding under the bridge maybe, black snakes gone cottonmouth or innocent water snakes taking the blame.

The barbecue piles smoked behind her.

The water lay low on the land, sealing spaces tight between the big, bearded trees.

An off-center V of ducks, pulling towards its short side, lost itself in the glare blurring any line between water and sky.

Her radio had turned Spanish or French.

And then, just as suddenly, the bridge bucked her up onto its hump, high above its waters, herded now, laked.

There were trees, but only lost and lonely ones, left living only that little.

And then, at the very top, high above the men in their little boats, she could see it, the Lake Charles Riverboat Casino, sitting back on its haunches, still a little uncomfortable in the lake, still getting used to the still.

The ducks came back and she remembered how her grandmother had taught her once that the way to know a bird's a duck is watch it fly because "if they don't flap they'll fall."

And she let go of having to push, let go of being pulled at, let the Falcon roll lazy down the bridge.

Johnson McCrae hurt. He was on the floor by his desk, sucking big haws of air, choking on the hee-hees.

Everybody who enjoyed *The Andy Griffith Show* loved Ernest T. Bass.

It wasn't like getting on a boat at all. She walked into a building beside the boat, like a hotel lobby.

"I'm sorry, dear," the woman said, "we've done all the hiring we're going to do. Why don't you take this complimentary chip and enjoy yourself?"

And then Ann-Mrie was sort of led through a line like for a Ferris wheel and she was indeed on the boat. In the casino. And she had that chip.

All she knew was blackjack, and only because she and Bobbi Martin had played it in school, except they called it 21.

Ernest T. Bass had already run off into his woods, into commercials, but even if he'd been running right into downtown Mayberry, Johnson McCrae would have picked up on this screen-two wonder.

She walked up, put down a comp chip, blackjacked, and walked away. Took her $12.50 and walked. Didn't take a drink even when the waitress from Houston, whose features weren't so sky in this new picture, explained drinks were comp, and what that meant.

It was the same black dress every girl from East Texas, South Louisiana, and West Mississippi wore when they came in looking for work.

Except it was different.

All the aerobics in those three states, the whole states, couldn't make a dress hang like that, like she didn't even know.

Johnson McCrae watched this different angel moving from one screen to the next, in different angles, watched her putting the whole place in slow motion, breathing into her hand like her chips were little birds to keep warm.

He wanted to hear her say something.

Then, finding herself in the nickel slots, she dug a nickel from her purse, dropped it in and pulled fifteen or twenty nickels out like she'd bought them. And walked out of the screen.

Except she didn't show up in the next one. Where she was supposed to. Out of the bottom left of two into the top right of three. But she wasn't there.

She was somewhere in between.

He jumped to his feet, trying to get into his shoes, going to go solve this mystery, and there she was again.

The riverboat hippo-jumped into its hourly voyage, required by law, around the lake, the motors like trucks way off on a wet night.

And she set her chips down and walked away.

When he got down there, the chips were gone. Somebody, and he'd known they would, had already gotten to them.

"Brenda, I need twelve-fifty right away."

"Coin?"

"Chip."

"Here you are, Mr. McCrae."

"Twelve dollars and fifty cents, Brenda, and I need one of the fives to be a comp."

"See *Matlock* last night?"

"No, Brenda."

"You ought to give him a chance."

He signed the cashier's ticket and was on his way out to the deck, Brenda still talking about Matlock being some sort of extension of Andy Griffith. He never gave that talk the first thought. You start listening at that, they can convince you of anything, that Gomer's better than Goober.

And he ran slam into her. Dropped a couple of his chips. Hit his knees like he was on a dance floor, "Sorry, I was looking for you," he said.

She didn't say anything.

"I was going to bring you your chips. You left your chips back there."

She looked at him from way back. From a different life, a different story. She looked at him from left field. From down the line. From across.

And she held out her hand, rubbing her chirping little birds in her fingers. "I went back for them," she said.

Showing her the painting was like dancing without music, was like singing for just the few, like telling the real truth. Took being quiet.

"What's it called?"

And somehow there was nothing that hard about that. Her being there made sense of the name.

"Ever wonder why people say pretty as a picture?"

And he had.

She touched the painting like a blind woman from the mountains of Guatemala come down to touch the face of Mary, tracing each stroke of his brush like it was sacred.

It seemed to him she moved in the very order he had, working herself around, or toward, up to, the yellow burst, which was of course all he could see.

She was playing in the purples and he remembered how he laid them out like a playground.

In the greens he recalled their growing, gathering, until she bogged down a bit in the browns.

But the reds rang of something coming.

And all that was left was that yellow, burning off itself like a summer-long brush fire.

Like brushed fire.

She looked at him.

"Nothing's pretty as a picture," she said.

Each morning Ann-Mrie Hunt would do the crossword and then read the classifieds. Jobs first. Then apartments. And call her mother, reading the very best apartment ads to her so she could comment on their suitability.

She knew how loud the sounds of him making toast were on the other end of the line.

Johnson McCrae would say, after she hung her mother up, "I just want to make you happy, Ann-Mrie," and she'd say how she just wanted to be happy.

She missed her dog. Ann-Mrie would sometimes sit down, and, staring right through the sun into the eyes of her grandmother, listen to her go on about Tick like she was singing, like it was a hymn about Tick. "The glory of old Tick at dawn," she'd sing and then hum a little until the wind pulled her away.

"What if I took a job in there?" she asked like she was reading the question right off the windshield.

"You don't need a job, Ann-Mrie."

"How do you know what I need? You said that place had good strawberry shortcake."

"Said best in this town. The only reason for anyone to have a job is to make money and I got enough for both of us."

"People do enjoy their work. Besides, Johnson, it don't feel right."

"What's that?"

"You giving me money."

"I don't give you money."

"Said you would," she said, rolling down the window, letting it all in on him.

"If you asked."

"Well, I wouldn't ask."

"If you needed it."

"Well, I don't need it."

"That's what I said."

"Dammit, Johnson."

An airplane flew low ahead, like it was going to land right on the highway.

Next night, staring into blank canvas, considering, seeing what could give way, Johnson said to Ann-Mrie something about a job at the casino.

It was right before spaghetti.

They had gotten to where they'd take turns making spaghetti, sparring with each other's family recipes, eventually making up new ones, even making up family names to go with them.

"Why's it the Willingham?"

"A Mr. Willingham took me and Daddy fishing once."

He made one of their faces.

"It's got fish in the meatballs, Johnson."

"Can't really taste it," he said at dinner.

"Wouldn't taste much like spaghetti if it did," she said, putting down her fork.

"Guess not."

"Would you want more fish in it next time, Johnson?"

Then he told her more about the job.

She told him how people'd say the only reason she got the job was because of him.

He said probably would, but if he didn't think she could do the job, then got up and looked out the window. The moon and sun were out there in the same sky together.

And then, as if it just occurred to her, she said to him, as if she was saying there was, simply, no sky, "Johnson," she said, "I been seeing somebody."

As if she'd said there's no ground there where you're standing, Johnson, those aren't even your legs.

And so Johnson McCrae walked around and people could see through him. And could talk about his insides.

And for the first time in at least a few forevers Johnson McCrae thought he should cry, but his eyes couldn't see that. Refused to look. Out or in.

He was just somebody, she'd said. It just happened. Just didn't mean anything, she'd said, but for Johnson there was nothing just in any of those justs.

But he still spoke them for her when he rode around thinking, felt sorry for her searching for reason in something that didn't make sense, that battled with his blood, and with his bones.

Only way out was for her to say Johnson, that's not what happened at all, but that wasn't going to happen at all.

He was helping his daddy hang drywall on the new townhouses that were starting to wrap around the lake.

When she first told Johnson he reminded her how they had talked about living in one of those townhouses. How nice it would be.

She said she still thought it would be nice. He laughed like he didn't think it was funny.

She told Johnson everything. Was the only way.

Even told him how Ty liked horses and country music.

That was how she first used his name. In the middle of a sentence like that.

Sometimes her grandmother would dance the top of the water, sometimes the tops of the trees. Sometimes she'd say if he only saw you in that dress.

If it rained, her grandmother stayed away and Ann-Mrie would watch the water rings on the lake and the flying fish flinging themselves free for a few feet. Struggle dancing, she called it.

And the casino took on grays. Murky blurs of moldy men and women milling about. No distinguishing, no division. Anything becoming anything.

His canvas said so. Without any help from him. Color was not needed. Wouldn't matter. So he let it be.

By now he'd seen every Andy Griffith enough that he didn't have to watch anymore. So he let that be.

And the words Ann-Mrie used meant so many things he couldn't make out what she meant. So he let those words be.

The day before Ann-Mrie told Johnson about Ty she told her mama about Johnson.

"Something about him, Mama."

She didn't tell her mama about Ty.

Nothing to tell except things mamas don't want to hear.

But grandmothers, especially ones who show up when they want, not only don't mind hearing about them, they'll bring them up.

"It's yellow-dress time, Ann-Mrie," she'd say, pretending like she wasn't there.

"But I told him about that boy."

"Because you love him. You tell Mr. McCrae you want him to carry you over to Beaumont after that dress."

And Ann-Mrie asked about explaining to Johnson about Ty, and her grandmother said all the explaining in the world won't make a man understand his woman with another.

"But," her grandmother said, "if he sees you in that dress, and you tell him how you love him, Ann-Mrie, don't say nothing about that boy ever again," and she began to fade, but brightened a bit and said, "You see him, smile—I'd smile, too—but you love Johnson McCrae."

So, back on the bridge that brought her, but in Johnson's car, him saying how he didn't see how this was any appropriate time to meet family, "One of These Nights" coming on and Johnson blasting it, Ann-Mrie did start to cry.

But then, after the song was over and the man was giving ball game scores, Ann-Mrie was still crying like everyone had lost.

After a while, Johnson asked, "You going to eat your chicken sandwich?" And he turned off the radio.

"Chicken wasn't meant to be eaten on a sandwich," she managed.

When they passed where she had stopped to buy gas she thought she saw the boy with all his rags looking out the window from between the oil cans.

But there wasn't a snake on the road.

The trucks went the wrong way.

She could sometimes make out the tight black lines along the ditches, stretched between crosses, but not on the road, not yellow ones.

When they got there Ann-Mrie's mother was sitting on the porch like she knew they were coming.

"My grandmother must have told her."

Johnson parked on the white grass where the Falcon used to sit.

"Mama, this is Johnson."

"I see it is. And how are you, Mr. Johnson?"

"Mr. McCrae," Ann-Mrie said.

"Fine," Johnson said.

"Huh?"

"It's his first name, Mama, you want to call him Mr. something, call him Mr. McCrae."

"But don't call me that."

"Just hug my neck, Ann-Mrie. Come sit down on this porch. Your daddy should be home soon, had softball practice, said he wouldn't be too late, but they lost the last couple and you know what that means."

"Daddy takes his softball pretty serious."

"Tea?" And Ann-Mrie's mother ran in the house without an answer.

"I don't know what to call her, Ann-Mrie."

The sun was as big as a softball.

"I call her Mama."

"What did your other boyfriends call her?"

"Didn't much."

"What would Ty call her?"

And it felt like, for both of them, the porch swing was going to fall from the ceiling.

"Tea!" rang out the door like the word had five, six, syllables, the last too high-pitched for humans, but Ann-Mrie later said how you could have expected tea dogs any minute. "You take lemon, Mr. Johnson?"

"Mr. McCrae, Mama."

"He told me not to call him that."

"Sure," Johnson said.

"Well, we'll have to run to the store for you."

"No, that's okay."

"If you take lemon.

"It's not a big deal, Mama."

"I just want him to enjoy his tea."

And Ann-Mrie's daddy pulled in.

"He's going to want a beer."

"Daddy gets to drinking when his team ain't doing so good. You can tell because he takes his hat off before he gets home."

"Cap," Johnson said.

"How do you know, Johnson? You ain't seen it."

"When they won the Big Thicket," Mrs. Hunt said, "I thought that thing was sewed to his head. Hardly drank a beer. Now look. Wish he'd grow up."

"Daddy, this is Johnson McCrae," she said, swinging her legs like she was on the playground waiting for him to come push her.

"Beer?" and Johnson took one. "We're just not hitting the damn ball," he said, like he and Johnson talked softball every evening, and he sat down on the porch step like he was giving the whole thing one last chance to work itself out. "Damn thing of it is," and he was rubbing his toe down deep in the dirt, his dirt, "it ain't a bad hitter on our club, we don't keep them around they can't hit the ball, but right now we'd have to get rid of the whole damn team."

And he spit. Right on his toe.

Johnson laughed.

"Johnson played professional ball, Daddy. A pitcher."

Her daddy got up, kicked the spit off his toe, looked one last time at his beer, crushed his can, and said, "Well, the only thing professional any of my boys ever done," his hand on the screen door handle like it was the handle of at least something, "is sell hogs or drive trucks, or maybe some welding, old Bobby damn Hawkins does some welding when he's not on his farm. Got one boy works on cars," and he swung the door back hard against its spring. "Works on them professional," he said and the door slapped behind him.

A bird flew up onto the porch rail like it knew Ann-Mrie's name.

"Daddy loves his softball," she said.

"Doesn't act like it."

"Yeah," she said, "that's the way he acts about what he loves," and she pointed up at the new moon and said, "Moons, Johnson, most things, they don't just fade out. They can fade damn in."

"You know, Phyllis Long teaches watercolor classes at our church, Mr. Johnson," Ann-Mrie's mother said when she came out of her bedroom at 10:30 the next morning. They picked at a plate of powdered donuts and drank Sanka.

She showed him a picture of a painting of a red barn she'd cut out of a magazine and said that's the kind of thing she'd paint if she was a painter, "Which I'm not. Don't have time for foolishness around here. You ever had anything in a magazine?"

He said he hadn't.

"What sort of work is that, Mr. McCrae, running a casino?"

"Wasn't anything I ever thought I'd end up doing."

"Everything I done is what I thought I'd end up doing."

"Seems like a really nice life."

She looked at him a long time. "Right after I met Ann-Mrie's dad, me and some girlfriends went to New Orleans," she said. "One of them had a cousin had moved there because of his homosexualness. We stayed with him in this little house with a fountain right in the middle of the living room. We drank stuff I never heard of and one night a man took pictures of me I've never seen." She turned the photograph of the barn upside down on the table and when Ann-Mrie got up her mother went into the bathroom for a while.

"She's got almost the same name as you," Johnson said, trying not to step on a grave.

"Yeah, but don't go by it," Ann-Mrie said, kneeling, touching her grandmother's marker where it said Anna Maria Day. "Went by Big Annie," she said, "and when Mama wanted to name me after her she tightened it up so I wouldn't be Big Annie, too."

"Always wondered what happened to your name."

"Didn't much happen with it. Started out that way." And she popped the rag at the headstone. Done.

And moved to the next one.

"How many do you do?"

She held up the bottle, half-full, said, "Until I run out."

"Probably should have listened to you about those sandwiches."

"Johnson, I ever tell you about my grandmother?"

"Told me she was your best friend. Told me about them drives you'd go on."

"After that, I mean."

"Told me she fell off the porch."

"After that, Johnson."

"Guess not, then. Guess you haven't told me about her."

Lying down beside his grave, Ann-Mrie worked on a man named Jebediah Martin's headstone, having a hard time with his 'J.' Once she got it she rolled over, told Johnson yellow dress and all.

And the wind blew new into the ground, trees leaning down, touching certain places.

"Johnson, I feel a cemetery is a park full of dead people." Ann-Mrie tossed the bottle up and caught it on a spin, looked around without moving her head much, asked him, "What you want them to do with you?"

"What do you mean?"

"Buried or cremated?"

"I tell you I look over this place, and you know how you say it's a park full of dead people? I can't help feeling it'd be a nice park for live people except for these grave markers," and he kicked one like a prickly tire on a new truck, and added, "clean as they are."

The wind was silvering, shining, and shrill.

"You'd have people playing across these graves? Children, Johnson? Picnicking? You'd have children eating on top of the dead?"

"Maybe I'd just bury them closer together," and he pulled his foot along the ground. "But you know, Ann-Mrie, it goes down a long way and I'm not sure we make the best of it skimming along the top."

"You'd bury people on the top of one another?"

He thought and said, "Maybe families or something."

"That's sick, Johnson."

"You don't think that, Ann-Mrie."

"That's what you want them to do, then? Pile them in on top of you?"

"You know," and he looked out across the highway at ground without dead people, marked ones anyway, and with that footing said, "you know, it don't matter. Don't make a damn."

"Never heard somebody come out and say they don't care what happens to them."

"Didn't say I don't care what happens to me. Said my dead body. When I die and my soul leaves, Ann-Mrie, I don't really care if they cut up my body and feed it to somebody's dogs. Serve some purpose that way."

"I want to be cremated, my ashes scattered at the Alamo. If you do it in 24 hours they don't have to embalm you. State law. Would you see to that for me, Johnson? Burn me in 24 hours? I don't give a damn for old Max Whipple poking around me."

"I'll try, Ann-Mrie."

"I'd do it for you."

"Would you do it for Ty?"

And the wind died right down.

"Fits."

"Ought to, it's my dress."

"Thought you wanted me to see how it looked on you."

"I didn't think it'd make much difference."

"Doesn't."

"God damn yes it does, Johnson, and you know it."

He walked out. Went out to the street. Two women walked by talking about the deficit.

Ann-Mrie came out. No yellow dress.

And she walked up to him and found his eyes.

He said, "See them women going there? Got it all figured out, but by the time they're finished talking about it from every possible angle, the USA is going to be even more in debt than when they started."

"She said it was time," Ann-Mrie said.

"You know, if that woman knew so damn much seems like she'd have told you something about Ty."

"She did."

"I mean beforehand, Ann-Mrie. Seems like she'd have told you I'd never be able to look at you, yellow dress or not, without seeing him touching you."

"I got three things to say, Johnson McCrae, and then do what you want, leave me to help with the deficit if you have to. First, Daddy won his game today, won big my grandmother told me. Second, the moon's so bright it's come out for the day. And you know what, Johnson? You might think I'm all in between you and that boy, but me and you, we're on this side."

And Ann-Mrie started doing jumping jacks.

"You look crazy, Ann-Mrie."

"This is my hometown, Johnson. They expect it of me."

The two deficit women stopped in front of the dime store.

"Not sure they're used to seeing you doing jumping jacks on their main street."

"Daddy calls them sidestraddle hops. Says they keep you from crying."

And Johnson McCrae stretched a bit, put his face into the new rushing wind, and started in with her.

THE LIGHT

When Victoria was born, her mother saw the Virgin Mary in a light bulb and folks came from miles around to look at the light and the baby. Her mother, Ruthie Anna, changed Victoria Lee's name to Victoria Mary when the baby was a week old, when what Ruthie Anna had seen in the light bulb had grown from a shadowy silhouette to a likeness so real it could've come out of a Polaroid commercial. And by the time Victoria Mary was two weeks old, her daddy, Tommy Ray, began to grow tired of his house being such a spectacle.

"Wouldn't be so bad if they didn't come over here Sunday afternoons," he said. "Everybody's got to see the baby, and they look at me like I don't have a thing to do with the damn kid."

"Don't you cuss our child, Tommy Ray," Ruthie Anna said. "She's a blessing to this house. She's holy." Ruthie Anna was at the living room mantle, arranging and rearranging the crosses, mangers, busts of Jesus, and 3-D Last Suppers they'd accumulated in the last few weeks.

She turned to Tommy Ray sitting on the couch across the room. "Honey, you're going to have to take down this rusty old gun. We're running out of room."

Tommy Ray's granddaddy, Mr. Howard, had given him that shotgun years ago, and it had sat on the mantle since. It wasn't coming down.

"Baby, you're pushing at me," Tommy Ray said. He looked out the living room window. Cars were slowing down like they do to look at Christmas decorations. He glanced at the TV, which never seemed to be on anymore. "I missed every ball game last week," he said. "By the time everybody got out of here, goddamn 60 *Minutes* was on."

Ruthie Anna said, "Ever since the miracle you been touchy like you don't want anybody to talk to you." She turned back to the mantle, then spun around to face him again. "And Tommy Ray," she said, "I've been thinking, and I talked to Mother and all, and we think it's best you stay out of Victoria Mary's room. I mean, especially if you're going to keep messing with the light."

Just yesterday Ruthie Anna had caught him trying to change the bulb.

Tommy Ray held his hands out to his wife, palms up. "Baby, don't you see? It's the way you say 'The Light,' when a few weeks ago if that bulb had burned out you'd have thrown it away like any other. If that light's so holy, you wouldn't all the time be so worried about it burning out."

Ruthie Anna had put a lamp in the baby's room for her and Tommy Ray.

She wouldn't even turn on "The Light" until a good crowd was worked up, eight or nine people, and then ever so gently, ever so careful. Each time she'd have to show where she saw the Virgin, and tell where she was lying when she first saw it. And always, sooner or later, she'd begin to tell how Tommy Ray'd been out hunting that day, and everybody would peek around the corner at him in the living room eating his TV dinner. He wouldn't look up, but he could feel their eyes on the worthless man who could've seen the Virgin Mary if he hadn't been out shooting birds.

It wasn't enough they thought him an unfit father. Hell, half these people didn't think he was the father at all—like Ruthie Anna was some kind of virgin herself.

Tommy Ray knew better that that. And now Mrs. Crawford, who'd never liked him anyway, ever since she caught him sneaking in Ruthie Anna's room in ninth grade, wanted Tommy Ray to stay out of his own daughter's room.

"Mama says the devil will use you as his tool to bring harm to

Victoria Mary."

"Dammit, Ruthie Anna, I'm not going to hurt my little girl," Tommy Ray said. "This whole thing's getting out of hand."

"Baby," Ruthie Anna said, and she smiled, "you know I don't think you'd hurt Victoria Mary on purpose."

That was enough for Tommy Ray, and he walked out. Somebody'd jammed a cross into the front lawn, and he thought about running slap over it but decided that might piss the Lord off directly.

After he'd circled the block, Tommy Ray drove down and bought a six-pack at the Pit Stop and sat and drank a couple in the parking lot.

Decided he needed a plan, needed to prove there wasn't any Virgin in that light at all and no matter what anybody said, his little girl was his little girl, plain as her mother. That was as far as Tommy Ray got. The plan kept stopping right there. He decided to have another beer.

He couldn't get over the idea that glow-in-the-dark crosses were running his shotgun off his own mantle, that Ruthie Anna and her mom were running him out of the baby's room, and he drank faster. Eventually he thought about taking the gun down himself and shooting Ruthie Anna and her mama dead in the ass, and he wondered how holy Ruthie Anna'd be then, how many people would confuse her with some kind of virgin.

He opened another and the beer went down smoothly. He was feeling pretty good and pretty angry at the same time. He twisted the radio on hard as he could, and Reverend Leon came blasting out at all the sinners. Tommy Ray took a big swallow and remembered Reverend Leon'd been in jail once. Johnny Paycheck or somebody'd helped get him out. Reverend Leon made himself a lot of money through Jesus after that. Didn't have to work regular hours.

Tommy Ray thought about regular hours and about Reverend Leon. He had to get out of his prison like Reverend Leon had got out of his—and he thought about Johnny Paycheck, and about paychecks, and when Johnny Paycheck and paychecks and regular hours and Reverend Leon and prison all came together, they exploded like a shotgun blast and it all became "The Light." And there it was.

The Lord, in whose service is perfect freedom. In whose service you learn to love your prison. In whose service you bring paychecks. And Tommy Ray finished the beer and opened a new one. He drank, and right then he became Brother Thomas of the Light.

Tommy Ray sipped another beer on the way home, drinking and counting. He'd start out asking an offering of, say, $1.50 to visit the home itself, and a lot more than that to turn on "The Light." He liked the name "The Light," but maybe it would be better as "Mary's Light." And the living room would be turned into a chapel, where a $5 donation would allow somebody to kneel before the mantle for prayer.

By the time Tommy Ray turned off the main highway he was into the Brother Thomas Television Ministries, direct from Hollywood. He opened his last beer, saying, "To the future," out loud to himself and his new partner, the Lord. He started talking all his plans out loud so the Lord could hear the future, too, and wouldn't be surprised when it came.

He swung by the Pit Stop for another six-pack.

He pulled into the driveway thinking swimming pools and bass boats, even a little Mercedes-Benz convertible for Victoria Mary once she got old enough to drive.

When he walked in the front door, imagining what it'd be like for the Pope to come by and suck up to him, Ruthie Anna was standing in the middle of the living room, cradling the blessed babe and crying like he'd never seen her cry before.

"It's dead, honey," she said, sobbing big little-girl tears.

"Oh my God, the baby," Tommy Ray said, falling to his knees, almost hitting the coffee table in front of the couch. He didn't care if he got hurt. He repented his ministry.

"No," Ruthie Anna said. "The Light. It won't come on. It's over. No longer are we blessed."

Tommy Ray got up off his knees, the beer swelling up in his throat. He couldn't think and he walked around the living room, sat down on the couch. He stood back up and paced around another minute.

Ruthie Anna kept crying and cradling the babe.

"Nobody seen it, did they?" Tommy Ray finally asked. "I mean, we can replace the bulb. Maybe it's the fixture's holy."

"No, honey," Ruthie Anna said. "The First Baptist Ladies Choir came to sing for Victoria Mary and when I went to turn on 'The Light' at the final chorus of 'Blessed Be the Tie,' nothing happened, baby. Nothing."

Tommy Ray held his head. It was all over before it started.

Later that night, God came to Tommy Ray in a dream. Told him the baby really was holy, folks just had to be made to see again.

The next morning, Tommy Ray was hung over and hung up. Dream or no dream, wouldn't nobody believe they were blessed now. All they had was Victoria Mary.

And then, there in the frying pan on the stove, Tommy Ray could see the glory.

"Honey, come here. I want you to look at these eggs. No, not at the white, baby. I want you to look deep in the yolk. You see? The three little crosses? See? Ain't that Calvary?"

SOME OTHER FIELD

I decided a long time ago if I can't play pro ball then the government'll just have to take care of me. Football was what I was good at. Worked real hard at being good at it and I ain't going to work hard at nothing else.

All I got to do is carry my paper around with me, make sure it gets signed, and be careful because a lot of folks will try to help me out. "Like to see you back on your feet," they tell me.

Just the other day that's what it was. Somebody's dad, said I went to school with his daughter, went on and on about some play I don't even remember soon as I walked in his hardware store.

He said, "Son, I'd like to help you out." Been calling me son for twelve years. Him and everybody else. You play ball somewhere, you're everybody's son. When he said that I went and sat down on his biggest Briggs and Stratton. It slowed him some, but he kept coming, "I could put you on the floor. You'd do right well on the floor." His shirt was yellow and his skin was almost as yellow as that. He used to smoke outside church.

The other fellow on the floor was cutting somebody a key.

"Don't want to much work on the floor," I told him, kind of surprised how I sounded. He just rubbed me wrong. Like an overexcited ref.

"Well, son, I mean I don't know what much else we got."

"Maybe this ain't the place for me," I told him.

"But, son, I would like to help you," he said, and he wouldn't let me leave until he called his buddy down at Lowe's and told him how I needed to get back on my feet, and they set up an interview for me which was good because I needed some new places. I was running out of them and I had done that before. I did it with the colleges.

Man, I had them my junior year. They would call Mama and be all nice to her and say things about how they wanted to "provide for my education" and how "fine a young man" she had raised, but then all that stopped on acount of my knee.

The schools that called me and Mama got smaller and smaller until they disappeared altogether.

I had my operation. I played my senior year, even, but there were some plays that I could have done something about, something a little different, and some of them schools might have come back, might have still said nice things to Mama. Coach said I was still the best he had coached, still the best in the conference, but I didn't have that same spring, that same potential to grow, that I did before my injury. That was supposed to make me feel better, I think.

So now, hard as I try to keep them off me, them plays will come make me take a look at them and then be gone. Sometimes, if I try like hell, I feel like I can change what happens, but they'll come back later same as ever.

The man from Lowe's called. Said he wanted to talk to me, why don't I come down one morning. Said that's when they hire, in the mornings. I had to put him off a couple of days because you got to pace this thing. Two people signing in one week don't do you no good.

When I did get down to the Lowe's this boy at the register said, "You here about a job, take home one of these applications and drop it off in the morning."

I told him I just needed to get my paper signed.

"You need to take home an application and drop it off in the morning."

I told him I didn't have much intention of being by this way in the morning.

"You need your paper signed?" he asked me.

The next morning I'm in there and the fellow I need to see's at lunch.

That same boy at the register said that even though it really wouldn't be morning when he got back, Mr. Lander had said he would talk to me.

"We usually only hire in the mornings," he said.

I didn't want to wait, but I needed that paper signed. I also was supposed to have Alice Moore's car back to her.

I called her.

She said, "You know I got to get Mama from the doctor."

I explained to her how her mama would have a better place to wait than I would.

She explained to me that I needed to get my sorry ass the fuck there with her car.

She was one of their specialists, one any woman would point out and say, "I'm proud the way she handles her men," one who had many, many ways of spinning you around the misery. She would cuss you out over nothing. And I mean out. In front of somebody.

If you tried to reason with the woman, she would say, "Son bitch sorry nothing dammit to hell horseshit motherfucker." My mama said she didn't have any qualms.

What would get her, what I finally figured out after days of trying to beat against the ugly wind, was to turn around and go the same way with it, and say, "Aw, baby, I hope I didn't hurt your feelings," or, "I see I've upset you." That'd get her.

"Baby, you're right," I told her. "I don't need to be hanging around here trying to get no job."

There was a moment of silence.

"You come get me, we'll get Mama, and we'll all go back down there together."

"Baby, I don't want your mama to have to come down here." I didn't want to be around the woman. I ended up having to promise that we would all cook dinner together that night, that I'd go shopping with them later, and that the next time I borrowed their car I'd get it back when I was supposed to.

Soon as I got off the phone with Alice, Mr. Lander busts in the door fat-belly happy from his lunch and says, "Bet it's been a while you had a good workout. Always wondered how one of you footballs would hold up unloading a lumber truck. It won't take an hour and a half if we bust it, then we'll talk about this job I got for you."

He had on them boots I used to get for my birthdays, long veiny muscles, and his cap wouldn't do like he wanted. He kept taking it off and putting it back on different.

He had me walking down one of them aisles with all the lawnmowers and we stopped in front of the work gloves and he said, "Go ahead."

I stood there.

He said, "Go ahead, now. Which ones you like?"

He meant the gloves. It hadn't occurred to me.

"I can't afford no gloves," I told him.

"I figured we'd give you those for helping with the truck. You're going to be needing them around here."

I wasn't going to be needing no gloves.

"What sort of position are we talking?"

"Position?" he asked me all smart-assed. "This ain't no football team, boy, this is a workplace. I know you need a hand. If a job will help you out, then I got something for you, but we ain't got no positions."

I was glad he didn't.

"Was kind of looking for a position," I said. I thought that had him. Was getting ready to put up with him telling me how I wasn't just going to find some position and how he was trying to help me and how it's hard to make something of yourself with certain attitudes.

"If you want to call it a position, well then, that's what we'll call it," he said, setting his cap so far back on his head the bill stuck straight up. "Rest of us'll just have to get used to holding positions, I reckon." This kind of made me lose a little respect for him, but mainly it meant I was going to have a hard time getting out of this job. And I could hear that truck backing up.

"Don't much like to work in the mornings." Something about him made me feel like he was one of them morning folks that look down on us that ain't.

"You wouldn't have to come in until eight." That "eight" was louder than the truck, but the truck was a lot closer.

"See, I like to sleep late," I told him. "Not many jobs will let you sleep like you want."

"Aw, we might have a position where you don't have to come in until two o'clock in the afternoon," he said, pulling the cap back down just a little and looking out at that truck.

"There are times when I might want to sleep on past two."

"What about a night job?" He reached down and picked out a pair of gloves for me.

"That's when most folks sleep, ain't it?"

He ended up signing my paper. I could hear him talking to the truck driver when I was leaving, but they were the ones out there on that truck in the sun when I rode back by with Alice, and I had on my sunglasses in the AC.

Boy, I used to could hit Barry Brown on this little slant over the middle without a thought. Now I think too much and drink too much with Uncle Cow, and I see Barry Brown at the Pic-Kwik. That's where he's working. Somebody tried to rob him a couple summers back and some way or another he figured out they didn't have a gun, I think. Anyway, he run them down before they got out of the parking lot. Everybody said for a while how Barry'd gotten faster since school, running cars down and all, but when I asked him he said the kind of running he did that night wasn't the same kind you would do on the football field, and so there wasn't much way for him to tell about that.

My mama won't hardly hug me no more. I mean if someone was to accuse her of it, of course she'd walk right over and give me one of them big ones just like when she thought she was getting a car out of Clemson. It don't gross her out or nothing, but she don't spend the time over me she used to.

I'd hate for her to hear me say that.

Used to, she wouldn't miss a game. Be there early. A bunch of them would have dinner down at the Quincy's and then stand out in the parking lot while the men took a last couple of swallows and made themselves one big cup with not a lot of ice in it to take in the game. Uncle Cow'd say, "They got ice in there."

I had been seeing Alice just about a month, and it had got to where folks were used to seeing us shooting pool with everybody on Fridays, and I guess she was, too. Anyway, what she wasn't used to was walking into Snoopy's and seeing me with the girl that had waited on us at Hooter's the week before. But she did, and the way she turned around and left out of there wasn't like she was going for good. It was more like an I'm-fixing-to-get-something kind of leaving.

So I followed her out to her El Camino.

"Baby, what's the matter?" I asked her.

"You call that little french-fry bitch 'baby,' too?"

And I said, real calm, "I ain't got but one baby. You know that. I don't see why you're so upset with me."

Well, then's when you could have been on the other side of the Bi-Lo parking lot and heard every word of my business.

She ended up leaving, but it wasn't the same kind of leaving she was doing before. I could tell she wasn't coming back. So I went on back into Snoopy's to explain how old Alice just don't always act right but that Hooter's girl, I think her name was Cindy, was sitting over in the corner with this fellow like she didn't have any pool left in her.

My daddy's after me to talk to Mr. McCormick about a job at his car lot. I'd be selling cars. He says my name around town, if I don't keep messing it up with my drinking and carrying on, could help me to sell new cars. I told Daddy I should be driving new cars now, and I thought for a minute he was going to come upside my head, but he said how once I'd been there six months they'd let me drive a demonstrator. I said how anybody can go down there any day and drive a damn demonstrator, and he looked at me for a few minutes and went and yelled at Mama.

Everybody thinks I can sell. All I'd like to sell is a good fake, bring them linebackers up one step, and hit Barry right in the numbers, stick it in his chest and watch him go.

Tonight I'm supposed to meet Alice to have a friendly beer, but I'm not sure what she means by that. Could mean she wants to bring up a bunch of shit that ain't the first bit friendly or it could mean she wants to have enough friendly beers to where we take our friendly asses back to the trailer and her car will still be there in the morning.

With me life's a lot like taking a nap. Sometimes I'll be laying there and, say, I won't have my arm just right, maybe I'm laying on it wrong or something. Well, generally, instead of moving myself,

I'll just lay there and try and make the best of it.

Uncle Cow says people like me and him are too lazy to get comfortable.

So I'll probably go meet her.

I didn't start the first two games my sophomore year, Del McCormick did, but we lost both and everybody said how Coach wasn't nearly as concerned about what Mr. McCormick would say if Del wasn't Tiger quarterback anymore. When he moved Del to wide receiver, everyone did a lot of speculating about how Coach probably told Mr. McCormick how much potential Del had over there at that position.

Of course I was aware of Mr. McCormick there on the fifty-yard line, and that he was already beginning to offer himself up as being responsible for the new Tiger quarterback, me, and I knew if I didn't hit Del at some point in the game, the first thing he would say to me in the locker room—he'd always be in the locker room unless we lost—was, "You going to have to learn to utilize your entire offense if you're going to grow." That meant throw the ball to Del.

There was this once, against T. C. Hannah in the third quarter, and we were up 13 to 6. This was my junior year and everybody on the team and most folks in the stands knew how I needed to hit Del at least once, that I hadn't yet.

I think T. C. Hannah knew too. Why else would they be paying a little more and a little more attention to Del McCormick? I didn't realize that then, though. All I could think about was getting the ball in his hands just once so that fat bastard in the stands wouldn't be the first thing I saw every time we broke huddle.

Well, like I said, looking back, they must have known that at some point in the game, for no apparent reason, I'm going to throw to #10.

I was ready to be done with it, and I send Barry out there, take the ball on a quick count, come up, and Barry's man had actually come off of him and was waiting for my pass. Luckily, he dropped it and soon as I saw that ball spinning on the ground I knew what I was going to do.

I mean I knew what I was going to do, but I didn't know what I was doing, didn't really have a choice. I'm not even sure I called a play. I can remember everybody looking at me weird when I said, "Ready, break!" but they, I guess because they didn't know what else to do, went up to the line. And Barry even came up to me wondering if this was going to be one of our special plays and I'm not sure what it was I said, but I do remember he smiled and went and set up. I sort of had that feeling that everybody on the field, except Del, maybe, knew what I was going to do. The referees, both teams, everybody on the field knew, and where that's something you don't normally want, it didn't so much matter, kind of made me feel better, like they were in on it with me some.

What I did, now this is third and seven and we're only up a touchdown in the third quarter, I take the ball and sprint hard right like some sort of option pass, but when I get out there, everybody in the stands had to be thinking I got nobody to throw to, and I'm sure Mr. McCormick was thinking that, but I did, I knew exactly who I was throwing to, and I sprinted even more, even closer to the sideline, and I plant, a couple of big boys bearing down on me, and just when Mr. McCormick stands up to see what in hell I'm doing, I turn and hit him right in his big car-selling gut. And it kind of stuck there and he put his hands out and there it lay. The football was in his hands.

Somehow or another we still won that game, mainly due to Barry as I remember, and nobody in our town ever said a word about that play. Every once in a while some fellow from another team would come up before a game, pat me on the butt and say something about doing them a favor and keeping the ball on the field. Mr. McCormick wouldn't talk to me anymore, but he would talk about me, how I was overrated and couldn't do what I do without this or without that.

I didn't throw to Del that next game or the one after that, I don't think, but somewere in there he started making himself get open and he might even run a few steps once he caught it. He wasn't Barry, but I threw to him some. And for the right reasons.

He called me. Del did. He called and said that it wouldn't be a problem, it'd be doing them a favor, that there was an opening on the used lot as we spoke, and I was kind of talking to him about it, I don't think I was really thinking of taking the job, just making it look good, and I don't know, maybe I felt a little bad about the way

I had been to Del in school so I was being nice. All of a sudden I can hear his old man in the background and then Del puts me on hold. When he comes back on he says how he hadn't known that the job on the used lot had already been filled. He didn't sound the same at all.

I was walking down to Pic-Kwik and I hear this three-tone horn working up close to me and when I finally turn to look, it's Mr. McCormick and he's got Del in the front seat there with him, but Del keeps looking straight ahead. It made me want to throw up. It was like the smell of my uncle's burned down house and I could even picture my insides, clean black like that.

There's this way I think that's not the way anybody else does. Maybe Uncle Cow, I don't know, but at night, after I've run through my plays, after I'm sure of what I should have done, if I don't try too hard, I can start to see me living on some other field, living the life I was supposed to, being able to keep trying at what I was taught. Once I'm locked into that life I can lay there and live there, sometimes until morning.

Once, Alice was staying over, and she had already fallen asleep, and I guess I was living in my other life, and she woke up and talked to me. She said I even felt different.

Things happen inside my head that most people don't have to worry with. I guess once in a while I'll hear something somebody says and it'll kind of be the same for me as them, but not all that often. Like you hear people say sometimes, when a song comes on the radio, "I was just thinking about that song," but they don't know it's going to come on. They ain't been trying to get ready for it, trying to catch it right when it comes on.

There are many stations inside my head. All they do is play music that I'm going to hear later. I can get ready for the songs and all they mean, but when they come on for everybody to hear, they hit me harder than linebackers ever did. I'm never really ready.

Used to, when it'd rain, Coach loved when it rained, we'd always practice late, run extra, do scalded dogs, but sometime in there, and it'd be just like I am with them songs, you'd know it was coming, but you'd never be ready, Coach would say, "I love you, boys," and dive right out in the middle of his practice field, and slide on his belly spitting mud and grass out his teeth, saying, "What's the matter, goddammit, don't you love me?"

And he'd get up and hit his belly again, "I said, I love you," and it was always hard to tell what he wanted you to do.

He'd get that way sometimes in a game, too. So fired up you wouldn't be a hundred per cent sure what he wanted. Every once in a while in the whirl of the game we'd break down. That don't hurt anymore.

What hurts are them plays where it was me that didn't keep it on an option, me that didn't sell the fake, where it was me that didn't call an audible, and the ones that do more than just hurt, the ones that live with me where I see my knee let them catch me, my knee couldn't make the cut.

Coach said to me, "Bennett, if all you had to do was stand there and throw it, every school in the country'd be after you. You'd be cat's ass."

If all I had to do was stand there and throw it. If that's all I had to do. Just stand there and throw it.

I got this little football, and I hung an old laundry basket on the light pole.

Fifty for fifty. Every day.

For a while Barry would come over and we'd run plays and then one day he said how it made him feel silly, that we were too old to be playing out in the yard, that people could see us when they rode by.

He did say he can get me two weeks' worth of signing down at the Pic-Kwik and he'll even take the paper up there for me.

Guess I will go see Alice. See what it is she wants. I know there are things she used to do that would almost make me forget.

And it's my fifty for fifty every day.

CANDLE SPELLING

Wheaton Smith sees.

On Sundays, when everybody gathers down at the school, waiting on Wheaton and his writings, waiting to speak Wheaton's message right out loud, that's what they say. How he sees.

"How else," they ask, a little burning in their own eyes, "does Wheaton spell with his candles?"

Because he sees, everybody says.

What's that mean?

He doesn't have to look.

What Wheaton's got is an old pasture on the hill, and this thing rolls, say, two football fields sort of side by side, maybe a little bigger, and he's taken by something's got him spelling things out in candles, and he says—hell, everybody says—how he sees, how he doesn't have to look where to put the candles. Just starts running around sticking candles in the ground. And then won't even light them all. Runs around pulling fire behind him, lighting this one or that at random, looking from down there the way a real shooting star must.

Then won't know what he's said.

Up here on the hill there's no making out the message. Close up it's pure fire. They say that's part of the mystery.

When the burning started a few years back Wheaton and his daughter Jess would drive all the way down and stand in the mayor's big front yard with the mayor and more of us each time, and everybody would read out loud the messages, try and find meaning.

"Charits falling," the candles read once and nobody knew what a charit was, even Wheaton, until he speculated how it could be chariots falling, like from heaven.

Another time he wrote, "Calvary shine."

Things that sounded like bad bible verses.

"A heart is a burning bush," one read, and, "Salvation upon our head," was another, and, "Tithe with love," too.

Everybody took something from what Wheaton burned on his hill. Wasn't there for just Wheaton, they'd say. God was working the whole area.

Then things started changing with the candles. With what they'd spell.

And somewhere along the line Wheaton started waiting until morning for somebody to tell him what he'd written, maybe let them buy him a coffee.

Then he quit coming down to see altogether.

Been coming to this, everybody says.

Should have known two back, they say.

Two back the candles read, "Jess wept."

"What was that?" they asked, and everybody said it must mean Jesus but wasn't any conviction.

Next one, "Love of a lamb," seemed sort of back to normal. At least that got said.

But then this last one.

"Blood of the kin." When we read that we stood there waiting for a 'g' on the end and the fire just went out.

That's why I come up here.

Thing is, Jessie left here a year ago. Went off to a college. Everybody knows what everybody thinks about that.

So what am I going to do? Knock on Wheaton's door, say everybody's worried, Wheaton, about what's been written? Ask him about Jessie? Straight out like that?

It's hard not to wonder about people that hurt themselves or whatever. Jessie used to pull her hair out. Nervous habit, everybody said, and they didn't have her to functions because she left plugs of hair around they couldn't even think about picking up.

It's hard not to wonder, much as you're not supposed to, what somebody's doing, what they're thinking. How hurting helps hurting.

One time I was visiting Jess and Wheaton and she told me she'd seen a bird fall out of the sky.

"Like a tear from the eye of God," she said.

Wheaton had buried the bird where nobody'd find it, but the dog dug it up and brought it to Jess warm as before. She put the bird in a bed in a dollhouse she got from the church one Christmas and used a toy stethoscope to try and hear the heartbeat.

She looked at me that day and said you listen so hard for things like heartbeats, all you hear's a listening sound, and I quit going up there until now.

Wheaton tells me, wait until tonight, he feels something needing said won't wait until next Sunday, says there'll be a message burning tonight'll make sense of all this.

Wheaton says, don't worry, Jessie's fine, he'll have her call.

Be nice to hear from her, everybody's going to say.

Wheaton says the fact the candles have brought me up here's reason enough to let them answer.

And I know it means he doesn't want me to ask him any more questions.

I do ask if my questions would affect what the candles say.

Wheaton says there's one big question so there's one big answer.

"Big as light," he says, and looks out over his land, gets that look old people get looking over their land, pieces of them and their clothes torn and left out there long ago, and I see candles burning in his eyes right there in front of me. Can't quite make out that they're saying anything, but his eyes have the moving part of fire perfect.

When I tell him I might wait up here tonight, see what it is the candles say, see what we both think, then talk maybe, he says no, there's no reading the candles from up here, go on down. He tells me don't worry what everybody'll say.

"What about the candles, Wheaton," I say more than ask. "Am I not supposed to worry about what they spell?"

Jessie's hair always had a mind all its own, and where a lot of people will fight hair like that all their life, Jessie played in her hair like slow rain falling. Before she started with her pulling it out.

What's left of Wheaton's hair somehow reminds me of that while he walks away.

"Done all the talking I aim to do," he says.

So here I go back down, knowing exactly what everybody's going to say, with no clue about those candles.

And I'm thinking how, when Jessie started cutting on herself, the whole town would hurt. She'd come down and do it. They said for attention but didn't give her any.

Come evening Wheaton's out earlier than usual, everybody says, and I think maybe it's a good sign.

He's one dot of fire up there in the early part of dark, like a scarecrow Statue of Liberty, until suddenly he breaks into his run.

And the talking starts. And not like it once was.

"Always looks like he's writing cursive but turns out print," somebody says.

"How's he know when he's done?" they ask and even, "What if everybody's to do that?"

And no making out the candles yet. Never much is until he's done, and he doesn't look anywhere near done, like he's going to have more letters burning words into the side of his hill than ever before.

"Looks like he needs a vowel."

And they run through their *Wheel of Fortune* jokes everybody's already heard so they don't have to give the whole punch line but do anyway.

"Maybe we should raise money for Little League by selling Wheaton vowels," somebody gets in just in time, everybody standing there, fire in our eyes, and somebody points.

But that's just it. There ain't nothing to point out. Or there's everything.

Like Wheaton's decided to erase it all, or better, he's marking through. In fire.

The smell of the smoke makes its way among us, stinging our eyes.

"Never been this bad before," everybody says, but we try to see something we've never seen over and over as the shapes of the flames form each other, from each other, over and over, sparking cinnamon stars and lots of thoughts, but nobody says anything else as the colors between orange and purple, shades we've only dreamed, hang in mid-air like nothing's black and white.

So there's this big paragraph of fire up there moving off the page.

Now nobody will say out loud what Wheaton wrote, like we're waiting for the grass up there to green, but what we're really waiting for is Jess to come back and do something with these goddamn ashes.

A REAL JOB

There's this friend of mine's a DJ. Still wears his hair the way he did in school. Drives the same car. Feathered back and Trans Am. Plays pretty much the same music.

Calls himself DJ Kyle Wild.

In the afternoons his voice connects the people of this town like somebody's bad news. And he knows it.

Down at the Holiday one night we're having a beer and these young ladies sit down at the table beside us.

Started out, before they arrived, he was telling me about something on TV the night before and using his little pinchy regular voice, but soon as they sit down he works himself into that DJ tone like he was growing into a bigger, deeper-voiced man right in front of me.

"We're talking about doubling power up to 20,000 watts," he said, about doubling his own power. "Have us reaching Fayetteville."

They weren't noticing him as much as he would've liked, maybe weren't from around here. "Means we'll add forty, fifty feet to the tower, have to put another light on it."

I didn't know what to say. Didn't know how to talk radio.

"Going after a bigger market," he aimed at them.

I caught myself nodding for him.

"Been doing thirty, thirty-five per cent, like to boost up to forty-five, fifty."

They weren't going to say anything. One gave him the least bit of a confused look.

"I'm in radio," he explained.

What he didn't explain, what he don't ever explain, would never talk so loud about, is his wife. She's stationed in Germany.

Wilma twirled baton in high school. Wasn't the kind of girl you'd have been watching her routine and said, "There's an Army career person, somebody going to see new, exciting places on Uncle Sam." But that's what she did.

I asked Kyle about that once when we'd both had enough.

"What made you want to go marry somebody fixing to head off to Germany?"

"Didn't know she was going," he said, like he was thinking about it for the first time.

But not hard enough for me. I said, "Seems like the kind of thing to tell you when you propose—love to get married but got this boot camp thing, little stint in Germany."

"Don't remember asking," he said.

"Proposing?"

"Not really."

I was thinking.

He was ordering another pitcher.

"How'd that get worked out then?" I went on.

"Just remember getting up one day and her saying we needed to set a date. Think I thought she was pregnant."

"Then she told you about the Army?"

"No, didn't tell me about that for a while."

"Probably should have." Life's one big day for Kyle.

"Yeah," he said, getting up, going over to their table, "but if you're going to be," almost saying 'married' out loud, sitting right down with them, "I recommend doing it this way."

He had turned that whole thing back on me, recommending something to me, here I was trying to help him.

But that was before everything was half the mess it got to be.

See, much as he likes to picture himself single, more than that he likes these young ladies running around town to picture him that way, and it's hard to keep somebody looking at that picture you find out your wife's coming home.

Barbara Roach was the only Roach girl left. I mean they were all around, still lived with their mama and daddy, husbands, and kids from all marriages, or most, but Barbara was the only one still wore shorts and wouldn't go out in her curlers.

And she thought Kyle pretty much single. Had her eyes on him. Let him have his hands on her. Enough to where Mr. Roach was ready to see his daughter married even if he didn't see deejaying as a real job, saw fixing cars as real work, the kind of work for his son-in-law. Had talked about counting him in on his old set of tools, and something about his own bay in the garage behind their house.

"Going to have to explain that you're already married," I said.

"Already explained I wasn't one night."

Wilma was coming in a week.

"Expect it's going to be hard getting used to married life."

"Just the wife," he said.

Next day he's down at the Holiday with a pitcher in his head and two pictures in his hand.

One he'd torn out of our old yearbook had Wilma smiling up at the lights, the field blue behind her, forever waiting for her baton to come back down.

The other was a Polaroid with something written on the back. She stood in front of a little tin building in her fatigues, sort of smiling but not the same smile spread across her yearbook picture. Like she finally figured out her baton wasn't ever coming back.

"That look like Germany to you?" he asked me.

"Wouldn't know Germany to look at."

"That's my wife in Germany."

"It's not like she's going to be walking around in that big old uniform," I started, but something about the red in her eyes made me say, "Of course it's Barbara Roach you need to talk to. Before Wilma gets back. I mean I wouldn't go trying to explain to Wilma when she gets here, I'd be married to who I was married to even if she did go be all she can be."

"Reckon I'll have to talk to the Roaches."

"Unless you'd like your own tools."

"Don't know the first thing about that kind of work."

"He's a big man to explain something like that to."

"And the only one can work on my car."

The week went by and I could hear in Kyle's voice he hadn't told Barbara Roach, or her daddy, a damn thing. He was avoiding me but couldn't keep me from turning on the radio and hearing those old pinchy sounds slip back into his DJ voice. Somebody riding down the road, somebody who'd gone to high school with us, might've been able to recognize him as Kyle from home room, not DJ Kyle Wild.

Everything he said went through what he was thinking.

He'd be about to give away some tickets or something and where he used to make the dog wash sound like something worth rushing to the phone for, now he made everything sound like it really was.

He'd just take the first caller and ask easy questions like, "What famous NASCAR racer drove car 43?"

Another day passed and people were listening to their tapes and CDs more.

Another and he wasn't even bothering to announce the request line number.

Another.

Wilma was going to be there the next day.

I went over to his apartment.

"Having dinner with the Roaches tonight," he said, not really watching Vanna White. "Think they expect me to announce the engagement before dessert."

"What makes you think that?"

"Mr. Roach told me that's the tradition. Said Bobbie and Brenda's husbands announced their engagements right before strawberry shortcake."

I didn't want to tell him what Vanna was turning around on TV. He'd see soon as somebody bought a vowel. It was a "before and after": SHOTGUN WEDDING CAKE.

Next day he's on the radio.

DJ Kyle Wild.

Best he's ever been.

You could see it all over town. People walking out of range of their radio right into range of their neighbors out washing their cars and things.

I called to see what happened, and he answers, "Sorry, we already have a winner," and hangs up.

I figure ain't that my luck. Didn't know it was a contest. Like Wilma and Barbara Roach.

I turned my radio back on and he's talking to some young lady about something going on down at the skating rink. She was giggling and he was playing it his best. DJ Kyle Wild.

He finally went to commercial and I called again.

"Can't really talk right now," he said. "Caught us at a bad time."

"Who's us?" I'm thinking, Wilma? Brenda?

"Why don't you meet us down at the Holiday this evening?" And he hung up, me still wondering who "us" was.

In fact, the rest of that afternoon he did every dedication, every commercial, and every throaty joke, me wondering who "us" was.

I'd feel like I had it figured out one way, that Wilma was coming home to a real husband, a DJ but a real husband, then there'd be something about the way he put his call letters and I'd know it was the other way, that DJ Kyle Wild was going to end up one of the grease-nailed Roach clan driving a wrecker around town.

Riding over to the Holiday I was still figuring.

Kyle was signing off, taking forever like he used to. By the time he said, "Don't touch that dial, you don't know where it's been," I was in the parking lot, as confused about "us" as from the start.

Decided I needed a pitcher before "us" got there.

Halfway into it I see Kyle's Trans Am pull into the parking lot but still can't see who "us" is. It takes longer than I thought it would, but, finally, "us" comes in and it ain't Wilma or Barbara Roach he's with.

She was the same girl from down at the skating rink, had a name started with an 'N'. Not Natasha but something like that. Said she's an ice skater, a figure skater. Said she only works roller rinks when she's in the South. When she finally went to the bathroom I asked Kyle was Wilma coming home married.

"Oh yeah," he said, sipping, "she's going to stay married, just not to me. Some fellow she met in Germany. Talked about him like he was real nice," and he pulled out that Polaroid. "He's the one took this picture."

"And Barbara Roach?"

"I barely got a bite of that good potato salad Mrs. Roach makes and Mr. Roach starts talking about me getting a real job, and I look around the house with the kids and dogs and that potato salad wasn't nothing like it used to be, and I get to looking at Barbara while her daddy's asking me what I know about transmissions, and she's looking more like her sisters, and he's telling me about valve jobs and timing belts and I get to thinking about all the broke-down cars in his yard and how he's supposed to fix them, and one of those kids jumps up in Barbara's lap and I'd just taken another little bit smaller bite of potato salad and it was even warmer and I thought I could see a little me in that kid in her lap and I didn't feel good."

"What about the strawberry shortcake?"

"Told Mr. Roach how I had deejaying in my blood, how I never expected to work more than four hours a day, and that was sitting down talking. Told him about *Billboard*'s article on the station and our format, how I was working toward a morning show, and tried a little of my morning material on him."

"What did he say?" I knew better than asking.

"Told his wife put the strawberries back in the deep freeze. Made the potato salad taste a lot better."

Nadia or Naomi was coming back and we both looked up at her.

He pulled his Polaroid out, looking at Wilma real quick. "She was some kind of pretty," he said, and as Nadia or Naomi got closer he put it back in his pocket, took a look at her, then back at me and, right when she's sitting down, asked, in full DJ Kyle Wild splendor, "Did I tell you we're adding another sixty feet to the tower?"

"Give you more power," I said, learning.

REDEMPTION CENTER

M om saves.
Dad delivers.

Mom's saved trading stamps since my birthday but doesn't know what for yet.

One place Dad delivers is the redemption center where Mom trades in her stamps. He knows when something good's come in before it hits the floor.

He'll tell Mom he delivered something like a croquet set, and she won't say anything, and I sit and watch Dad dream about us out back playing croquet or whatever came in that day.

Now he delivered a computer to the redemption center. "Whole thing in one box," he said.

Mom didn't say anything, just raised her eyebrows enough to notice.

He didn't have to say what he was thinking, but he did. "Computers never done anything for me but make me work harder." He looked right at Mom and said, "Up to now."

Coming out of the grocery store once, Dad stopped in the exit. Holding the door, he looked down at his feet and said, "Used to be a mat you stepped on to open the door," then looked at the money still in his hand, and said, "People counted your change out and gave it to you where you could do something with it." He said, "Computers do the counting now." He said, "Do something with computers, Son."

Every once in a while he takes me delivering. Some people are nice and some act like I'm not there. One guy I always ask can I stay in the van, but I guess it's the bad section of town. The guy makes me sit in his office with him while Dad unloads, but he won't look at me. He drinks coffee and farts like I'm not there. He watches a TV on a cardboard box, shows I've never seen, like he picks up different stations than us and in different colors.

A little dog scrambles around under his desk like part of the man's foot.

"Lap dog without a lap," Dad said once.

"Mean bastard," I said, and he didn't say anything about me cussing.

So I asked Dad did he ever think of doing something with computers.

He said, "They didn't have them until it was too late to make a difference in my life."

There's football players older than my dad, but he always acts like his life's over like that.

I asked him why Mom doesn't want to get the computer at the redemption center.

"Never likes to stop saving," he said, "but I think it's her hair."

I didn't know how her hair'd have anything to do with a computer.

He said, "Ever since she went to that place in the mall that puts your face up on a screen and a computer decides your best hairstyle."

I told him that was supposed to help.

"The computer matched her up with a style that looked good on TV," he said, "but when she came home she looked like her whole head had grown."

I told Dad I didn't remember noticing that.

"Me neither," he said, "but a computer did it to her."

The redemption center's not like a store. They get one item in and when it's gone, when somebody redeems stamps they've saved for it, it's gone. Might not ever get another one in like it. I've seen bikes and TVs come through, lots of lawn furniture, but this is the first computer.

I told Dad that and he didn't say anything.

He's got a way of talking with Mom I don't. He says the same about me, but it's hard to tell what he means and what he's saying for me.

When I tried telling him, he said I'd better not try to figure that out.

"Think about what you think about," he said.

But I can't think about everything I think about. It has to start somewhere.

Last night we went to Dairy Queen and on the way home pulled into the redemption center parking lot. They had set the computer up in the show window with a cardboard family looking at the screen, pointing and laughing, but it's just a picture of their selves they're looking at.

Mom saw that picture, and that picture of a picture they were pointing at, and put the last of her cone in her mouth and said, "Mmmm-hmmm," and Dad drove off.

When we got home he went out to his garage and turned on his music.

Dad told me Mom used to listen to the same music, but you'd hardly know. Now she turns anything not Christian off, or down where it might as well be.

Then, every once in a while, a song comes on in the car and Dad'll turn it up, and she'll just roll down her window. Longer she sits there, letting the wind at her hair, looking off somewhere, the more I imagine her like that all the time.

Last night Dad said, first thing when he sat down for dinner, "Saw some people looking at the computer." He'd been delivering a box of Swiss Christmas ornaments.

Mom said pass the bread, but I didn't.

I said, "We ought to get the computer."

She looked at me and I felt horrible but good. Her hurt looks had hardened a place in me that knew stating my opinion did not have to devastate her.

She walked around the table and got the bread herself. On her way back barely tapped the top of my head with the bottom of the breadbasket and knocked what good I was feeling right out of me.

We've got computers at school. I could show Mom how to run one.

Dad can run most anything, but I can't imagine what he's going to do. Download music, maybe. I hope not porn. If Mom caught him she'd put the computer in the yard, and I worry how she'd feel.

I like to travel.

During library period I go to China and the moon and all the way to other galaxies. I think that scares Mom. I try to understand, but I think all the belief in the world don't do you good if the way you believe is not let yourself know better.

Mom's not one to talk to that way, though.

Today I heard Mom talking in the kitchen and I wasn't sure she was on the phone until the long quiet gave it away. I knew it was Dad when she said, "I can't think of one thing a computer'd help me do."

I didn't hear her hang up but after a while gave up listening.

I sat thinking how a computer could help her.

Could organize the bills, but we don't get enough to matter. "Just enough to keep us in our place," Dad says.

There might be a way a computer'd make money, like a web-cam, but I don't think Dad in his underwear's going to bring in much. Mom in hers, maybe, but I haven't seen her underwear, even in the laundry, in a few years.

I wondered if Mom might be able to sell crafts or something, but I couldn't handle having all that crap around.

I decided maybe she's right. Maybe there's not much a computer could do for her.

When Dad got home he told me about calling Mom.

I told him I knew. "Not budging much on the computer, huh?"

He said he was calling because he'd be late. "She brought up the computer," he said.

So there's hope. Thing is, Mom's so in love with hope she hates to see it die one way or the other. And the longer Mom's determined not to redeem for the computer, or for anything for that matter, the more Dad thinks it costs him.

When she walked in he said, "This computer's the first opportunity I've had in a long time," looking at her like she's in charge of handing out opportunities.

I realized one day the kids at school must think I have at least one computer at home.

They think I'm pretty smart now.

I know I'm smart, and I know there's something out there that explains what my family needs, and if it's on a computer it's because somebody put it there. A computer may not show us, but getting one means we're willing to look.

Today, after school, I rode by the redemption center. A woman looking at the computer waved through her own reflection on the window. I wished I had parents like her, or even like that fake family in the picture. Not so my parents weren't my parents, but so they liked things like computers.

I looked at the family in the picture, pointing at themselves, and decided Dad needs something to blame things on. I looked at that woman's reflection and knew Mom needs her world, her family, me, to be something she understands.

The woman touched the computer, light-fingered, then walked up to the counter and pulled a pile of full stamp books from her purse. Before I pushed down on my pedal, though, she walked over to this big barbecue, big enough to cook forty hamburgers at least.

Standing there with her hand on the grill she kept looking over at the computer.

Sitting on my bike I felt balanced between what I wanted her to do.

I wanted her to be a barbecue lady so we could be a computer family, but I was getting nervous about wanting at all anymore. I realized I was happiest when I didn't think about things, like when I ride down the hill near our house.

If that hill was long enough, I'd be happy the rest of my life.

Still, when that lady rolled the barbecue to the counter, I got that shiny feeling inside.

On the way home I rode down my hill. About halfway down, I let go of the handlebars and coasted. The first song I ever knew the words to came into my mind for the first time in a long time. I sang "Hey Jude" out loud all the way to the "na-na-na-na"s and coasted until I was going so slow I had to grab ahold. I stopped and stood still and waited for the dog that chases me, but he never came.

Dad told me when he was my age teachers and people would tell him do something with computers, but he could never figure out what they meant for him to do even if he found one in the street.

He told me his dad bought an adding machine with a sort of display and called it a computer and wouldn't get rid of it even once you could buy one smaller than your hand at the dollar store.

He looked at me and said, "When I was little everybody remembered getting their first television."

I started to tell Dad people don't change much, but that's probably what he meant. I can't figure out if he knows what he's doing. He'd say don't worry about that, that's thinking about the wrong thing.

Maybe that's the answer. Maybe what you think makes you happy. Maybe that's the difference in a family like the one in the picture in the window and us. Maybe that's what he's saying.

I don't know if I want that, though. It'd be like always knowing where you're going.

When I ride my bike I don't just coast down my hill. I like ending up behind things and above things. I like to lay my bike beside a bush and lay down by it and wake up and not know where I am.

If I told Dad how I think, it'd be like that.

They moved the computer. It's still in the window, so they haven't given up on someone redeeming for it, Dad says, but they've got an entertainment center in there, too.

This big piece of furniture with a TV, a VCR, and a place to keep videos costs less books of stamps than the computer.

I'd just as soon Mom not find out about this, or thinks it's ugly if she does. Trying to figure out what she likes is hard, though.

This Christmas I've realized her bible's beat up pretty bad. It was her mom's and has old church programs stuck between the pages.

When I turned twelve Mom stopped waking me up on Sundays. The first few weeks felt like the beginning of summer, but one morning I heard her leave for church and I didn't want to go with her, but I wanted her to want me to.

I watched the ballgame with Dad and kept looking at him in his sweats, watching the clock for her to come home so he could have a beer. I felt like we were that fat, farting guy with his little dog, and I finally asked why he didn't go to church with her.

"One day she quit trying," he said.

Of course that got me thinking.

My mom laughs a lot more in my memories than in real life. Still, I prefer the real mom. Maybe it's because I can touch her if I want, but I never do. Maybe I'm thinking she might see the mom in memories, realize she doesn't have to give up anything to get that back.

When she does laugh, in the living room or the kitchen, it sounds like she's somewhere like church or the principal's office, laughing like she's not supposed to, can't control herself, and if you walk in she'll stop like you caught her. Every once in a while, though, walking in on her makes her worse, and she loses herself laughing until you join in, even though you don't know what you're laughing at. You're just laughing.

I try to think about it that way when she's crying, but it's harder to hear your mom cry, and I only made the mistake of walking in on her crying once. That haunts my memories.

Today at school the computers locked up so I didn't know what to do besides read books.

I thought about the words written in the books, and wondered which ones were read. I thought about all the books in all the libraries in the world. There must be a lot of words not read, like in hardbacks. All their meaning not there.

I looked at the dead computers and knew words floated out there somewhere, more than could fit in all the libraries in the world.

I thought so long I didn't finish the story I was reading.

When I got home, Dad was there early, in his garage with his music and the door locked, and I got a weird feeling in my stomach.

Their bedroom door was closed, and it was so quiet I knew Mom was in there.

Those two rooms are on opposite sides of the house and there's nowhere to go I didn't feel in the middle, so I went for a ride.

I headed for the hill. I tried not to think about the computer, or getting Mom a bible, but sometimes I have to work through stuff to get to the place only I know about.

It helps to sing, not just in my head but out loud, opening up my mouth and pushing words into the wind in my face, and it helps to let go of the handlebars, but I can't always do that.

Mostly I have to let that place sneak up on me, like I've never been there before.

When I'm there, though, it doesn't feel real or like a dream, like the wind might feel with nothing to blow, with no way for anyone or anything to tell it's there, and no way to stop.

When I was little and we'd go somewhere in the car I'd ask how much longer and Mom'd say, "If you don't stop thinking about it, it'll be forever." So I'd stop thinking. When we got where we were going I felt like two moments meant to be far away were side by side.

When we stopped going so much, I got my bike.

The dog at the bottom of the hill, I never know when he'll come or from what angle. And when he doesn't come at all, the next time he's there like it's my fault.

I call him Mix-Up because of how he feels about me. The first time he chased me I thought he'd bite my leg, maybe pull me off my bike, and he ran along growling and barking like the meanest damn dog in the world, and all he had to do was turn his head and snag my ankle as it pedaled by, but he never did.

He ran with me like that enough it got fun. I looked forward to seeing him. Talked to him alongside me.

This time, though, he turned and grabbed the toe of my tennis shoe and his head circled around with my foot a few times. Finally, we came off the pedal and he let go.

He shook himself. I stopped and rubbed my toe. We stood there looking at each other until he walked away like someone called him he didn't want to come to.

I told Dad about getting Mom a bible. He couldn't tell what to think and I wasn't going to tell him, just looked at him like I didn't have anything to hide.

He asked me how I'd go about getting her a bible. I thought how I've seen Christian supply stores in strip malls but never been in one, and how they never carry bibles at the redemption center. I thought maybe people buy bibles through their church.

I said I'd get him to buy her one. "You love her," I said.

I thought he was going to cry, so I told him Mom loved him, too.

We sat there long enough that's all I remember. Don't remember getting up. We're just not there anymore.

I took Mom's old bible down from the mantle. The pages were coming apart. She used to have it out every night, turning pages and marking scripture, but I knew she'd only use her bible for church now to try and keep it together as long as possible.

On the inside cover her mother wrote, "Through the Word I'll be with you forever."

There's more words in that book than any I've seen, but her Mom called it the Word. That means something. Holding onto her bible I decided I can know something means something without knowing what.

I looked at the church programs between the pages and thought how they meant whole Sundays to Mom and what meaning she must've taken from those sermons.

I knew Mom would always want her bible close to her no matter what it took to hold it together.

I thought about how Dad delivers so many computers to so many places, but never bibles anywhere. "Not one box," he told me. I thought about the words in all the books and computers in the library, and I realized computers have bibles.

Mom could keep her old bible on the mantle, and for church, she didn't need another carrying bible, and she could use the computer to study scripture, maybe get more out of the meaning, understand some of the hard passages.

A computer, I decided, would help her through the trials of being a Christian in a computerized world.

And maybe, I told her later, a computer'd help me and Dad see the light, if it's not too late.

"God works in mysterious ways," I said.

She looked at me and for the first time in a long time it didn't seem like she was saying something she was telling herself to. "I'll go in for redemption," she said.

I said, "Mom."

She opened her eyes wide like she was trying to see something and said, "He sure is mysterious."

And when she says 'He,' the God 'He,' you hear her capitalize the word, but this time with her eyes so open there was room for Dad coming through the door, and me, too, and her smile smeared across her face until her laughing included us and we laughed with each other and at each other and we laughed every sort of laugh we could laugh until we woke up the next morning with sore jaws and we looked at each other, and we laughed some more and somehow we ended up in the backyard and we didn't have a big barbecue or a croquet set, we didn't even have a computer yet, but I took the garden hose and chased Mom and Dad all morning.